Jeremiah S Mcgregor

Life And Deeds of Dr. John Mcgregor

Jeremiah S McGregor

Life And Deeds of Dr. John McGregor

ISBN/EAN: 9783744754101

Printed in Europe, USA, Canada, Australia, Japan

Cover: Foto ©Raphael Reischuk / pixelio.de

More available books at **www.hansebooks.com**

LIFE AND DEEDS

OF

Dr. JOHN McGREGOR,

INCLUDING SCENES OF HIS CHILDHOOD, ALSO SCENES
ON THE BATTLE FIELD OF BULL RUN, AT THE PRIS-
ONS IN RICHMOND, CHARLESTON, CASTLE PINCKNEY,
COLUMBIA, SALISBURY, ON THE BANKS OF THE JAMES
RIVER, HIS ESCAPE, HIS RETURN HOME, THE TRAGI-
CAL SCENE ON DYER ST., AND THE HEART-RENDING
SCENE AT THE CITY HOTEL IN PROVIDENCE, WHERE
HIS EVENTFUL LIFE TERMINATED.

BY

JEREMIAH S. McGREGOR.

FOSTER:

PRESS OF FRY BROTHERS,

1886.

PREFACE.

The life of a public man is a leaf of History. It is a leaf also in which minute facts, and particular causes, and personal transactions, are brought out in such strong relief as to have the effect of a picture taken from the Great World, but viewed as we view small portions of the firmament through telescopic glasses. Such lives are essential elements in the great picture of Humanity in action. We must see the heads of the actors, as well as the great moral of the actions, which together compose the drama of human society.

The life of Dr. John McGregor is such an element in the history of our last war. It cannot be separated from the great struggle

with the South. Men may take what view
they please of him, or the acts in which he
was engaged; but some view they must take.
Many of his acts were no trifling parts, nor
performed in an unimportant period, of American progress. They were brilliant points on
the battle field of Bull Run. They moved on
from that bloody field to those loathsome
Southern prisons. They made part in the
terrible scenes at Richmond, Charleston, Castle Pinckney, Salisbury, and on the banks of
the James River, terminating in a tragical and
heart-rending scene on Dyer Street, and at the
City Hotel, in the city of Providence. In all
these scenes, whether of war or peace, the acts
of John McGregor cannot be separated from
History. My duty is to place the lineaments
of a public character on record, where they
may be seen by all observers, and left, undis-
figured, to the final judgment of posterity.
This duty the writer has undertaken to
perform with strict fidelity. The records of

the country, happily, furnish the foundation for
most of his statements; the testimony of eminent and honorable gentlemen, themselves
actors in some of the scenes described, fur-
nishes other materials; and, finally, the papers
and narratives of private persons make up an
aggregate of facts and evidence amply sufficient to satisfy the demands of Truth and
Justice.

These facts the writer has undertaken to
compose in a clear method, an easy narrative,
and, as far as he has the ability, an agreeable
style. Beyond this he does not seek to go.
He would neither exaggerate the objects in
his picture, nor add a coloring beyond the
hues of nature. Nor has he need, for the
scenes through which the doctor passed, have
interest enough without any distorted figures
drawn by the pen of Fancy. In fine, the
writer desires to make a volume of authentic
and unimpeachable history. It will aid the
historian who, in future time, shall wish to fill

up his page with the actors and actions of our days.

The life of a man whose mind was so concentrated on Surgery, Physical Science, and the art of medicine, is one in which the lover of those sciences cannot fail to take deep interest. It is but natural that men will seek to know the origin of one who stood in the foremost rank with the most noted Surgeons and Physicians of Rhode Island and Connecticut, and the facts of his early life, and of the expanding of his mind. With eager curiosity we look back, and in the sports of his childhood, in the pursuits and occupations of his youth, we seek the origin and source of all that is noble and exalted in the man, the germ and the bud from which have burst forth the fair fruit and the beautiful flower; and we carefully treasure up each trifling incident and childish expression, in the hope to trace in them some feature of his after greatness. Feeling that the early life of a man like John McGregor,

and the growth of those feelings and opinions
which afterwards embodied themselves in the
art of Surgery and Medicine, would be interesting to many, we deem it fortunate if we can
give even a short sketch of his life. We will
give a short account of his parentage, and then
content ourselves with a general outline of his
after life, so full of striking events and useful
labors.

LIFE AND DEEDS

OF

DR. JOHN McGREGOR.

The grandfather of Dr. John McGregor was one of the lineal descendants of the McGregors of Scotland. He was born in Dundee, Scotland, in 1743, and died in Coventry, R. I., in 1820, aged 77. In coming to America, he brought with him little except a liberal education and a thorough knowledge of military tactics. His knowledge of military tactics made him a desirable acquisition to the ranks of the yeomen of Connecticut, who were vastly ignorant of the first principles of military art and strategy. Here he drilled a large company, in Plainfield, in military tactics and evolutions, and hurried with them to Boston at the first alarm which convulsed the feeble colonies at the prospect of so unequal a struggle. He afterward commanded his company at the battle of Bunker Hill, and was in many of the principal engagements during the entire war of the Revolution. He was present at the surrender of Cornwallis at Yorktown, and was finally honorably discharged by Washington, at New York, at the end of the Revolution. He was in command of the guard over the lamented Major Andre during his short confinement, and ever related the incidents attending his trial and execution, with uncontrollable emotion. He married Betsey Shepard, daughter of Simon Shepard, of Plainfield. She was born in Plainfield, Connecticut, in 1757, and died in Coventry, Rhode Island, in 1815, aged 58.

Col. Jeremiah McGregor, son of John McGregor, and father of Dr. John McGregor, was born in Coventry, Rhode Island, in 1780, and died in Coventry, in 1875, aged 95. He married Elipha Nichols, daughter of Major

Jonathan Nichols. She was born in Coventry, Rhode Island, in 1784, and died in Coventry, September 9th, 1874, aged 90.

The late Dr. John McGregor bore the name of his grandfather, and was born in the town of Coventry, Rhode Island, on the 10th day of October, 1820. His earlier years foretokened those of his manhood. Among his neighbors, he was always called a good boy, and among the boys of his age, he was the great favorite. In all their projects, he was the preferred one who was commissioned to carry them forward to their consummation. His early education was only such as our best seminaries afforded at that time.

We will pass over his boyish days, or until he arrived at the age of sixteen. At this time his character is described by those who well knew him, as distinctly formed. He was full of hope, and animated by a just sense of honor, and a generous ambition of honest fame. His heart was open and kind to all the world, warm with affection toward his friends, and with no idea that he had, or deserved to have, an enemy. It seems that he was intended for one of the learned professions. In the spring of 1837, we find him engaged as clerk in the store of Stephen Taft. At this time, Stephen Taft was one of the largest manufacturers of cotton cloth, in the country. His village was situated in the east part of Coventry, where now is located one of the largest and most beautiful cotton manufacturing villages in Rhode Island, called Quidnick. After serving as clerk in the store for about two years, he returned home, and soon after placed himself under the teachings of Andrew Cutler, of Plainfield, Connecticut, then quite a celebrated man. Cutler was a graduate of Brown, Rhode Island, and, at that time, was keeping a High School in Plainfield. After studying one year with Cutler, he occupied his time for the next two years in keeping district schools in different towns in Rhode Island.

In 1842, he became a member of the Phenix Baptist Church, at Phenix, R. I.; and all through his life he exerted his influence in the furtherance of the cause of Christ.

At the time the Smithville Seminary opened its doors to the public, he was one of the first to enter. He pursued the usual preparatory studies, and graduated in 1843. Smithville Seminary commenced operations October 14th, 1840. The members of the Board of Instruction were as follows: Hosea Quinby, A. M., Principal; Stowell L. Weld, A. M., Associate Principal; Caroline L. Johnson and Amey M. Baxter, Teachers in the Female Department; Stephen B. Winsor, Register and Steward. This institution was located on the Hartford and Providence Turnpike, nine miles west of Providence, in a very pleasant country, and stood on a small eminence commanding a view of a few neat villages, and also three places of worship situated near.

In 1843 he entered the office of Dr. William Hubbard, of Crompton, Rhode Island, as student. He continued his studies with Dr. Hubbard three years, attending medical lectures at the Medical Institution at New York, within that time. I shall always remember the first time that he went to New York to attend medical lectures. At this time, a number of young students, who were going to New York to attend medical lectures, had an understanding among themselves to meet at McGregor's old homestead, and go to New York together. In the afternoon previous to the day appointed for them to start for New York, Moses Fifield, Thomas Andrews, William Bennett, Wilbur Briggs, and John Hill, arrived at the old homestead of Dr. McGregor, and found him making preparations for the journey. The evening was passed mostly in conversation concerning their future plans and prospects. Some one of the party, I think it was Bennett, asked the writer what profession he should choose. In reply, he told him that he thought a certain trade would be as profitable as a profession, and that he thought he should learn that trade. "What trade is that which would be as profitable as our profession?" asked Bennett. "Making coffins," answered the writer, "for I think that when all of you get through with your studies, and commence to practice, there will be great call for them."

That was before the Hartford and Providence Railroad was built, so those young doctors were conveyed, by carriage, from the old homestead to Central Village, on the Nor-

wich and Worcester Railroad. From there
they went, by rail, to Norwich, and from Norwich, by steamboat, to New York. Where
are those men to-day? Fifield is at Center-
ville, Briggs in Providence, their hair as white
as the driven snow; and the others are sleeping
that long and dreamless sleep, in their graves.

Dr. McGregor graduated in 1845, at the
Medical University of New York. Soon after,
Dr. Wagstaff offered him a situation in the
Lying-in Asylum of New York. Dr. Wagstaff
had the full control of that institution at that
time. Dr. McGregor remained in the institution until 1846, when he returned to his native
town. He opened an office at his father's
house, and notified the people that he was at
their service. The following is the

NOTICE.

Dr. J. McGregor, a graduate of the New
York University Medical College, having, for
the past eighteen months, enjoyed the facilities
for the acquisition of medical knowledge which
the New York hospitals, asylums, and dispen-
saries present the medical student, feels himself
qualified for the discharge of those duties which

devolve upon a medical practitioner. He has located himself at his father's house, where he can be consulted at all times, when not professionally absent.

JOHN McGREGOR.

NEW YORK LYING-IN ASYLUM, March 22nd, 1845

I certify that John McGregor, M. D., of Kent County, Rhode Island, has been District Physician to this institution for a year past, during which time he has attended a large number of women in confinement, and had charge, in my absence, of the Asylum; in the fulfillment of which duties he proved himself an attentive and skillful practitioner of the highly important branch of practice, Obstetrics.

WM. R. WAGSTAFF, M. D.,

Resident Physician of New York Lying-in Asylum, member of Parisian Medical Society, Lecturer on Midwifery etc.

When it was announced that he was coming home to settle, all the people were pleased, and ready to receive him with outstretched arms. He had been at home but a short time before he had more business than he could attend to. His rides were very long, for there was no doctor within eight miles of him. He had no fear of competition, but those long rides over those large hills, through storms and dark nights, were not very pleasant. His home soon became a hospital, where the blind re-

ceived their sight again, cataracts vanished like
the morning dew, hair-lips were remodeled into
very respectable looking ones, crooked eyes
were straightened, polypuses were removed
from the nose; legs which had been drawn up
for years were straightened, cancers were
removed with the knife, and many other operations were often performed.

Dr. George Wilcox, of Providence, commenced the study of medicine with him at this
time. Here it was that Dr. Wilcox first dis-
sected a human body.

The ruling motive of McGregor's life, was
to become an accomplished surgeon. From
his start, all his energies were bent in this
direction, and finding a country practice did
not afford him the facilities he desired for the
prosecution of this branch of his profession, he
removed to Phenix. This change was against
the wishes of many of his warm and true
friends. He did not leave his friends and
patients until he had engaged Dr. P. K.
Hutchinson, a young physician who had graduated with the greatest honors which the
medical institutions could bestow, to take his

place.   Dr. Hutchinson became one of the
most eminent physicians in the country.   Dr.
McGregor moved to Phenix in the fall of
1847   Here he was surrounded by factory
villages in all directions. He had previously
scanned this section of country, and came to
the conclusion, that with his knowledge of
surgery, this was the place for him; for hundreds, every year, were injured in those
mills. Here his expectations were more than
realized. He proved himself to be a surgeon
and physician of no small merit.   Here he
gathered around him a host of true and reliable
friends.   When a man could truly say that
such men as Joseph Lawton, Henry D. Brown,
Elisha and Thomas Lamphear, Simon H.
Greene and family, James B. Arnold, David
Pike, William C. Ames, Cyrus and Stephen
Harris, and a host of others, were among his
true friends, he should be very, very proud.

The doctor early showed his Scotch blood;
that is to say, he had the strong, substantial
qualities of character for which the well-trained
families of Scotland are remarkable.   No
people are calmer in action, more reverent in

religious feeling, or surpass them in integrity.

In July, 1848, he married Emily P. Ames, daughter of William C. Ames, of Phenix, Rhode Island. I will not attempt to describe, in detail, all which transpired concerning him while he was at Phenix; for it is enough for my purpose to say that his practice was very extensive, and that he was very successful in his surgical operations, which were his specialty.

In 1850 or '51, Dr. Bowen, of Thompson Hill, Connecticut, was summoned by the Angel of Death to the Heavenly Court, beyond the clouds. He was one of the most eminent surgeons in Connecticut. His practice was very extensive, and he was very successful in operating. The loss to the people was very great. There was a vacancy to be filled. "Who can fill Dr. Bowen's place to the satisfaction of the people? who will dare take his place as surgeon?" were the sayings of many of his friends. All who know the people of Thompson, know that doctors and preachers of the gospel must be first-class, to be patronized by them. After receiving a number of letters from some of the most prominent men in

Thompson, soliciting him to come and take the place left vacant by the death of Dr. Bowen, he went and made a thorough examination of everything appertaining to the filling of the vacancy. He was convinced that he could, after a time, fill the place to the satisfaction of Dr. Bowen's friends, and the community at large. After coming to this conclusion, and consulting with his wife and her family, and many of his most intimate friends, he concluded to leave Phenix, and to go to Thompson. It was a great trial for him to leave Phenix, and his many warm friends; and it was as great a trial to his friends to have him go. He moved to Thompson in 1852, and soon opened an office, and commenced practice. We will drop a vail over the sad hearts which he left at Phenix, and follow him to his new field of operations.

The wealthy and beautiful little village of Thompson, with all the adornments which wealth can add to make it attractive to the eye, is situated on a gentle eminence which slopes toward the setting sun, terminating in a beautiful valley, with Quinnebaug river

glancing and dancing through it; and faced
by Woodstock Hill, whose echo sends back
the sounds of its clear-toned bells. Such is a
glimpse of Thompson Hill.

Here we find Dr. McGregor, surrounded by
the most hopeful prospects. Everything which
makes life desirable seemed to be placed before
him. Dr. Bowen's friends received him kindly,
and his practice soon extended far and near;
and ere long he could truly say that his success
was far beyond all for which he had ever
hoped. At this time, to the beholder, he was
in his zenith; but man's vision does not extend
far into the future. We are visitable by many
things which make life enjoyable, and also by
things which make life almost unendurable.
The vicissitudes in this life are many. Ere
long the bright blue sky was o'ercast by a cloud
which filled his heart with anguish and sorrow.
His beloved wife was taken sick, and in
March, 1855, her soul passed from earth to
that undiscovered country. Then, all was
darkness and gloom. His home was desolate,
his fairest prospect blasted. Sympathy will
often soothe the feelings, but will not heal the

heart which is lacerated and torn. He knew
that everything which could be done to alleviate her sufferings, and to defeat the Angel
of Death, had been done as far as it was in his
power; and he also knew that he must submit
to the all-powerful and all-wise God. The
mortal part of his beloved wife was carefully
removed from her home in Thompson, to
Phenix, her own native village, and the scenes
of her childhood, and there, beside her kindred,
laid away to wait the coming of the Lord.
Sadly he returned to his desolate home.

I will now pass to other scenes. The scenes
in this life are ever changing. We see him
driving over those lofty hills, and through
those fertile valleys, through storms and pleasant weather; exposed to the cold in winter, and
to the scorching rays of the sun in summer.
The many varied and difficult operations which
he was called upon to perform, and his uniform
success, made for him the reputation of a first-
class operator. Windham County had unlim-
ited confidence in his ability; and the suavity
of his manners endeared him to every household
he ever entered.

As time passed on, he formed an acquaintance with Elizabeth C. Allen, a lady endowed
with all the qualities requisite for a physician's
wife; and, on January 10th, 1856, they were
married.

I will pass on to 1861. At this time it could
not be denied that the United States was a
great nation, although a controversy between
the North and South had grown to an alarm-
ing extent. The sympathies of the people were
divided between the Northern and Southern
parties, on the great question. A war, which
so many of the warm spirits of the country
looked for, was soon to take place. At this
time the Great Rebellion was inaugurated,
and had begun to convulse the land. The
tocsin of alarm was sounded, and the notes of
preparation were heard from Maine to Louisiana.

On April 12th, 1861, the rebels bombarded
Fort Sumter, and caused Anderson to surrender it into their hands. Then the North was
obliged to take up arms against the South.

In the controversy of this exciting period,
the doctor was, in his opinions and acts, with

the Republican party. He was educated, believed, and acted, according to the political
principles of Abraham Lincoln.

The revolution through which the American
nation was to pass, was not a mere local convulsion. It was a war for the rights of the
working class of society, and against the usur-
pation of privileged aristocracies. The time
had come for a great and decisive struggle
between these two parties.

Three days after the fall of Sumter, President
Lincoln issued the memorable proclamation,
calling for seventy-five thousand volunteers to
defend the national Capital, and, finally, to
recover possession of the United States forts,
arsenals, and navy yards, which had been taken
by the rebels. Previous to issuing that memorable proclamation, President Lincoln had
done all that mortal man could do, to appease
the angry South. He spake to them with voice
majestic as the sound of far-off waters, falling
into deep abysses. Warning, chiding, he
spake in this wise: "Listen to the words of
wisdom, listen to the words of warning, from
the lips of one that loves your. I have given

you all the privileges which the Constitution allows you; why then are you not contented? why then will you be rebellious? I am weary of your quarrels, your wranglings and dissensions. All your strength is in your union with the North, all your danger is in discord; therefore be at peace, and as brothers live together." But they heeded not the warning, heeded not those words of wisdom.

The greatest excitement was created by that proclamation. The doctor said to all the people whom he conversed with, upon that matter, "I cordially concur in every word of that document." The doctor, true to his impulses, was a patriot, stern and inflexible; and the sudden and urgent appeal to arms, stirred him as with the sound of a trumpet. In the morning, after reading, in the morning paper, the full account of the bombardment of Sumter, and the President's proclamation, he said to his friends, "I feel that I am in debt to my country, and I am ready and willing to discharge the obligation." Noble and high resolve! He immediately wrote to Gov. Buckingham, offering his services to his country. He soon received a dispatch from the governor, stating that he was pleased with his offer, and that his services would be gladly accepted, and that he would be appointed surgeon of the third regiment.

At this time the State Legislature was not in session. Gov. Buckingham, however, had such wide financial relations as enabled him immediately to command the funds for equipping the military for the field. Connecticut, I think, may say with honest pride, that no men went into the field, better equipped, or more thoroughly appointed and cared for.

When a man in the doctor's position, was ready and willing to leave his home, his friends, his large practice, and almost everything which makes life desirable, to enter the army, and to be subjected to all the sufferings and hardships of war, others were ready to follow his example. He never would encourage men to do what he dared not do himself. His motto was, "Men, follow!" He did no more than thousands of others were ready and willing to do, at that time. It is to men who possessed such hearts, that the country owes a debt of gratitude; for by and through them the country was saved. What would this country be to-day if that terrible wave of rebellion had not been broken? It was broken, and thoroughly broken; but at what a sacrifice!

The preparation of the third Connecticut regiment, which was then almost ready to start for Washington, was similar to that of other regiments which were at that time preparing for war; and the scene at Dr. McGregor's at the time he left his friends and home, to join his regiment at Hartford, was similar to many other scenes of the same nature, which were taking place in many other sections of the country. The parting scene I will not attempt to describe. I will leave that to the imagination of the reader. It is enough for my purpose to say that the farewell had been spoken, and he was on his way to join his regiment. As the last glimpse of his home and the dear ones vanished from his view, a peculiar pensiveness seized upon his mind. There is an indescribable charm that links one to the land of his nativity. As he took the last view of his home, the thousand endearing friends and objects left behind, rushed upon his mind like an avalanche. Tender emotions swelled his bosom. It was then he set a true estimate on all he had parted with. Then, for a few moments, the interests of the future were lost in the melancholy of the present. Such, no doubt, were his feelings.

I will not burden the reader with the particulars of the momentous journey from Hartford to Washington. The regiment, on arrival, immediately went into camp, with the understanding that a forward movement would take place very soon; for the rebels were massing their forces at Manassas Gap. A full description of those tented fields, and the doings of those seventy-five thousand men, previous to the time when the word, "Forward!" was sounded along the line, would be interesting to the reader; but I do not feel competent to give it. An old soldier, standing on Arlington Heights, and viewing the tented fields,—one who had seen much service in the army, who had fought the Indians all through the Florida war, and who had been in many of the hard fought battles in Mexico, said, as he surveyed

those fields, "Those poor boys little know what
they will have to suffer, and to contend with.
War is a terrible thing, only realized by those
who fight the battles. I know that those
Southerners will fight. I have been with many
of them in many hard fought battles. I speak
from experience." That old soldier was Gen.
Winfield Scott.

On the 22nd of May, Gen. Butler took command of the department of the South, and made
his head-quarters at Fortress Monroe. On the
10th of June, occurred the battle of Big Bethel.
But a still more serious lesson was to be learned
by the people. During this time, the rebels
were not idle, but were spreading their field of
operation, taking possession of important
points, massing their troops at different places,
and preparing to make an assault on our Capital.

The 4th of July dawned with all loveliness. But what a scene presented itself to
view! The panoramic view, presented to the
beholder, as he stood on Arlington Heights,
was such as man can never fully describe. As
far as the eye could reach, the country was one

vast encampment. An army of seventy-five
thousand young men, the flower of the North,
was preparing for the great struggle. The
most noted lawyers had left their courts and
clients; the most eminent surgeons and physicians had left their patients; cashiers had left
their banks; manufacturers had left their
mills; farmers had left their farms; clergymen
had left their churches; governors had left their
states in other hands; professors of colleges
had left their collegians; clerks had left their
offices; mechanics had left their shops; and
volunteered, as soldiers, to put down rebellion.
Such were the men who were tenting before
Washington.

The day soon dawned, when the beholder
could plainly see that something uncommon
was taking place in that encampment. Staff
officers were dashing from head-quarters to
head-quarters; the tattoo was beat by the
drummer boys; the high notes of the bugle
were sounded throughout the encampment; the
boys were falling into line; tents were taken
down and packed; and everything denoted a
departure of the army. Soon the word "For-

ward!" was sounded along the line; and then
came the sound of tramp, tramp, tramp, mingled with the clatter of the cavalry, and the
rumble and jar of the artillery. As the long
line wound itself over the hills and out of sight,
the burnished guns and other implements of
war glistening in that July sun, a sadness
enveloped those left at our Capital, who, on
bended knees, were asking God to protect
those boys, and to save our country. Then
the stillness became almost oppressive.

With anxious hearts, we waited for news
from the front. We received a letter from the
doctor, while the army was at Fairfax Court
House, and another when it was at Falls
Church. That was the last one we received
from him, before the battle of Bull Run. His
letters were full of hope. He believed that the
North was in the right; and he also believed
that right would prevail. He was always
hopeful, from boyhood. We knew that the
two armies were in close proximity to each
other; and we also knew that our army was
then at the very mouth of the rebels' den. We
knew that a terrible battle would soon be

fought, and we were very anxious to have tidings from our army. Still we watched and prayed.

On the 19th of July, the telegraph wires fairly trembled, as they conveyed the news to all parts of the country, that the battle had begun. Then, all was excitement, for we were then living between hope and fear. I will leave to the imagination of the reader, the feelings of the people, when the news of the battle of Bull Run first reached them. The tale ran thus: "The Northern army is routed, the rebel army victorious. The Connecticut and Rhode Island regiments have suffered fearfully. Slocum, Ballou, and many other noted men from Rhode Island, and a large number from Connecticut, lie dead upon the battle field. The second Rhode Island and the third Connecticut are almost annihilated, and Dr. McGregor and many others taken prisoners."

A true panoramic view of that battle field, at the time when the battle was at its height, would be such as few would care to see. The armies of the North and South had faced each other, and wrestled together, for eight long hours, with that desperate courage which Americans only can show. I will give you a short account of that terrible battle which made Bull Run and the plains of Manassas famous for all time.

The day was bright and beautiful. On the right was the Blue Ridge, and in front were the slopes on the north side of Bull Run, crowned with woods in which our army had early planted its batteries, and all around were eminences on which were posted small but anxious knots of spectators. The hill above Mitchell's Ford is almost entirely bare of trees, and sufficiently high to afford an unobstructed view of the opposite heights. The guns of the enemy, on the opposite hills, were plainly to be seen with the naked eye; and the heavy clouds of dust, rising above the woods, in front and on either side, indicated the direction in which the heavy columns of the enemy were marching.

The night before the battle, it was generally understood that the rebels were gathered in great force, and designed turning our left flank, which rested a few miles above the scene of

Thursday's engagement, at a ford on Bull Run, called Stone Bridge.

On Friday, the 19th, Gen. Joseph E. Johnston, who had the command of the army of the Shenandoah, posted at Winchester, arrived at Manassas Junction with four thousand of his division, to re-enforce Gen. Beauregard. The remainder of his army, with the exception of a sufficient force to hold Winchester, was intended to arrive on Saturday. Gen. Patterson was ordered to swing around Winchester, and to hold Gen. Johnston in check. The noted Edmund Ruffin, who had against the walls of Fort Sumter fired the first defiant gun, had come to this conflict, with his flowing white locks, and with eighty odd years weighing upon him, to take part in this fight, encouraging his young men by his presence and example. Agile as a youth of sixteen, with rifle on his shoulder, his eyes glistened with excitement as he burned to engage the Yankee invader. It was Gen. Beauregard's purpose to make the attack instead of waiting to receive it, but he preferred at last to let our army take the initiative; perhaps for the reason that Gen.

Johnston's division was detained at Winchester. Gen. Burnside's brigade was situated on a hill, above the stone bridge, and the Connecticut troops on his left.

At eleven o'clock our batteries opened fire, with rifled cannon and shell, on their left, without response. We heard, away to the right, about three miles distant, the heavy booming of cannon, followed immediately by the rattling crack of musketry, the discharges being repeated and continuous, which notified us that the engagement had commenced in earnest at that point where the battle was to be fought and won. Beauregard and Johnston commanded their main body at Stone Bridge. Gen. Jones's brigade was stationed at Blackburn's Ford. On the east side of the ford, we had two strong batteries in a commanding position. Jones's brigade made an attack on our left flank, but their troops were compelled to retire with heavy loss. All the morning, we had been bombarding Gen. Longstreet's position in his intrenchment on the other side of the run. We pressed their left flank, for several hours, with terrible effect; but their men flinched not, until their number had been so diminished by the well aimed and steady volleys, that they were compelled to give way for new regiments.

At two o'clock, the result hung trembling in the balance. We had lost many of our distinguished officers, and our ranks diminished fearfully. The rebels had lost heavily. Generals Bartow and Bee had been stricken down; Col. Johnson, of the Hampton Legion, had been killed; Col. Hampton had been wounded; but there were at hand the fearless generals, Beauregard, Johnson, and Longstreet, to contend with. Our generals were still hopeful; but the musketry on our side was getting faint; and the great guns of the enemy, unprovoked from our almost exhausted batteries, were now but sparely fired. Everything, therefore, indicated another lull; and it could not be made certain to our minds but that we had really won the victory, after all, and that the last cannonade was but the angry finish of the enemy.

Suddenly a cry broke from the ranks, "Look there! Look there!" and, turning their eyes

towards Manassas, the whole of our drooping
regiments, as well as those who were moving
to the rear, saw a sight which none who gazed
upon it will forget. A long way up the rise,
and issuing from the enemy's extreme left,
appeared, slowly debouching into sight, a dense
column of infantry, marching with slow and
solid step, and looking, at this noiseless dis-
tance, like a mirage of ourselves, or the illusion
of a panorama. Rod by rod the massive
column lengthened, not breaking off at the
completion of a regiment, as we had hoped,
but still pouring on, and on, and on, till one
regiment had lengthened into ten. Even then
the stern tide did not pause, for one of its arms
turned downward along the far side of the
triangle; and the source of the flood, thus
relieved, poured forth again, and commenced
lining the other in like manner. Still the
solemn picture swelled its volume, till the ten
regiments had doubled into twenty, and had
taken the formation of three sides of a hollow
square. Our legions, though beginning to feel
the approach of despair, could not take their
eyes from the majestic pageant; and, though

experiencing a new necessity, were frozen to the sight. The martial tide flowed on, the lengthening regiments growing into thirty thousand men, with a mass of black cavalry in its center; the whole moving toward us, as the sun danced upon its pomp of bayonets, with the same solemn step. This was war, compact, well made, and reasoning war. It was war, too, in all its pomp and glory, as well as in its strength; and we at once comprehended we were beaten.

Gen. Patterson had let Gen. Kirby Smith slip through his fingers, with his thirty thousand; and the tide of battle turned in their favor by the arrival of Gen. Kirby Smith from Winchester, with his fresh thousands; and our Waterloo was lost. Among the last to turn their faces from the fight they had so gaily sought, was the Burnside brigade, which, accompanied by Gov. Sprague and its gallant Brigadier, and headed by its colonels, retired in line of battle with orders to cover the retreat.

As I am not writing a history of the war, I will give a description of scenes, only where the doctor was one of the actors. The first reliable information we received concerning the doctor, after the battle, was by a letter from Alexander Warner, Major of the third Connecticut regiment. The following is the contents of the letter.

CAMP KEYES, WASHINGTON, Aug 1st, 1861.

Mr. J. McGREGOR :

Dear Sir,

Your letter came to hand last evening, and I hasten to give you the information you desire. Your son, Dr. McGregor, was surgeon of our regiment. The morning of July 21st, he went with his regiment to the battle field, and there stopped at a house which was to be used as a hospital for our wounded. He remained there through the day, faithfully attending to his duties. When the retreat was ordered, I rode up to the hospital. The doctor came to the door, all besmeared with blood. I told him that a retreat was ordered, and, for his own safety, he had better leave at once. He asked me if there was any preparation for removing the wounded men. I told him there was not. He then turned and went into the hospital. As he turned, he said, "Major, I cannot leave the wounded men, and I shall stay with them, and let the result follow." That was the last time I saw him, and I did not know what had become of him until, a day or two ago, a prisoner, belonging to the fourth Maine regiment, made his escape from Manassas ; and he saw the doctor there, attending to our wounded men. I have no doubt but that, in due time, the doctor will return to us. I am very happy to be able to give you the above information, as to the whereabouts of your son; and anything I can do for you, in relation to him, I shall be most happy to do. We miss the doctor very much, as he was highly respected by all of our regiment.   I shall see the doctor's wife as soon as I get home, and give her all the particulars.   If there is anything I can do for you, in any way, please let me know.

    Yours very truly,
        ALEXANDER WARNER.
           Major of the third Connecticut regiment.

The part of his history while he was a prisoner in the rebels' hands, and the account of his sufferings while in those loathsome prisons, and of the many scenes in which he was one of the actors, are written from a description which he gave himself. His account of his imprisonment, his trials, his sufferings, and of some of the blood-curdling deeds which he saw done, is as follows.

First, after our army was ordered to retreat, many of our regiments passed within view of my hospital. It was a lonesome time for me, I assure you. Seeing our army retreating, and knowing that very soon I should be surrounded and taken prisoner by those rebels whom I despised, was not very pleasant, to say the least of it. Very soon I could hear the rebels shouting, "Victory!" and soon on they came, more like demons from the infernal regions than civilized men. About this time the 69th New York regiment, a regiment of Zouaves, commanded by Col. Michael Corcoran, came marching along, all in good order; but you could see by their movements that they were terribly disappointed. You could also see, that if they were obliged to retreat, they would not run like a flock of frightened sheep, but would retreat like men who had been trained to obey orders.

On came the howling rebels, flush with victory. Soon that noted Black Horse cavalry came rushing down upon these Zouaves. It was the most splendid company of horsemen I ever saw. Every horse was as black as the raven's wings. Every man showed that he had been trained by a master of no small intellect. They were armed to the teeth; and their horses were beautifully caparisoned. I learned afterward that that company was composed of rich men's sons, and it was really the flower of the South.

The 69th, on going on to the battle field, had disrobed themselves of everything except their pants and fighting utensils, which made them

look rather peculiar. They, also, were armed
to the teeth, and as no other regiment was
armed. I remember how those long saber-bay-
onets glistened. I knew those men knew how
to use them, as well as those long sheath knives
which they carried in their girdles. I had seen
that regiment go through with their peculiar
drill, and I knew that whatever company
attacked that regiment would suffer. The
69th was composed of men selected for that
particular regiment. They were the worst
men that could be found in the city of New
York. At least, such was their reputation.
They were allowed to fight according to their
own peculiar way.

When I saw that splendid company of cavalry swooping down upon that regiment of
Zouaves, I knew that there would be a terrible
battle. Instead of forming a square, as most
regiments would have done, to protect themselves from the charge which that company
of cavalry was soon to make upon them, they
opened ranks and let those horsemen ride right
in among them. Then came a scene which
can never be fully described. Then those

Zouaves showed their peculiar mode of fighting. Within two minutes, the two regiments were all mixed up, each man fighting on his own hook. This was just what those Zouaves wanted. They had been brought up in just such scenes. They had been drilled in that mode of fighting. They were in their glory now. Now was the time when those knives became useful. Horses went down as by magic; riders were unseated for the last time. In less than twenty minutes, the ground was covered with the dead and dying,—men and horses in one promiscuous heap.

THE BLACK HORSE CAVALRY.

We waited for their coming beside that craggy run,
And gaily shone their trappings and glistened in the sun.
We saw the well kept horses and marked the stalwart men,
And each Zouave his long knife took and tried the charge again.

On, on they came in close set ranks; O, 'twas a goodly sight!
Their horses shone like ebony, their arms were burnished bright.
A breathless silence: then there came a ringing down the van,
"Lie low! Remember Ellsworth! Let each one pick his man."

A thousand rifle flashes; then shrieks and groans of pain,
While clouds of dust uprising over the fatal plain,

While the gleaming bayonets seemed like the lightning's flash.
A cry, "Remember Ellsworth!" and the deadly forward dash.

Silence;—horses riderless and scouring from the fray,
While here and there a trooper spurs his worn steed away.
The smoke dispels—the dust blows off—subsides the fatal stir.
Virginia's Black Horse Cavalry are with the things that were.

A wailing on the sunny slopes along the Shenandoah;
A weeping where the York and James' deep rolling torrents pour;
Where Rappahannock peaceful glides on many a fertile plain.
A cry of anguish for the loved who ne'er may come again.

The widow clasps the fatherless in silent, speechless grief,
Or weeps as if in flood of tears the soul could find relief.
The Old Dominion weeps, and mourns full many a gallant son
Who sleeps upon that fatal field beside that craggy run.

O matrons of Virginia! with you has been the blame.
It was for you to bend the twig before its ripeness came;
For you a patriot love to form, a loyal mind to nurse;
Yet ye have left your task undone, and now ye feel the curse.

Think ye Virginia can stand and bar the onward way
Of Freedom in her glorious march, and conquer in the fray?
Have you so soon the truths forgot which Washington let fall.
To cherish Freedom ever, and Union above all?

Go to! for thou art fallen, and lost thy high estate,—
Forgotten all thy glories; ignoble be thy fate!
Yet from the past's experience a lesson may be won;
Though all thy fields be steeped in blood, still Freedom's march
       is on.

The South was, on that day, taught a lesson which they never will forget. Col. Corcoran, and most of the living Zouaves, were taken prisoners. Months after, I had a chance to study his character. I was in the same prisons with him, and shared the insults and privations of the necessaries of life, while in those prisons.

Soon after that fight between the Black Horse cavalry and the Zouaves, my hospital was surrounded, and we were all taken prisoners. A strong guard was placed around, and then I realized the value of freedom. At the time that Major Warner rode up to inform me that a retreat was ordered, Lafayette Foster, United States senator from Connecticut, was in my hospital. He had been helping me nearly all day. When he heard me say that I should not leave those men, he turned to me, and said, "Doctor, what shall I do, go or stay?" I advised him to leave immediately, for I did not consider that it was his duty to stay. He shook hands with me, and said, "Doctor, be hopeful. Good by." He was the last man whom I spoke with from the North, except the prisoners, for many months. Night came on.

I watched over those poor wounded men all
night, doing what I could to relieve their suffering. Before morning, a number of them
had passed from earth. I did not once think
that our army would retreat so far. I expected
that the battle would be renewed on the next
day. How anxious I was to hear the booming
of our Northern cannon once more; but when
the next day closed, and no sound save the
groans of the wounded and the jeers of the
rebels, I felt as if all was lost. I will mention
a few incidents which occurred while I was at
that hospital, and then I will pass to other fields
and other scenes.

An officer belonging to the regiment of
Zouaves known as the Ellsworth Zouaves, was
brought into my hospital. (The reader will
remember Col. Ellsworth was shot in a hotel
at Alexandria, by the proprietor of the hotel,
named Jackson.) This Zouave officer was
mortally wounded, and, on the following day,
he died. Soon after his death, a man, or rather
something in shape of a man, came into the
hospital. I learned afterward that his name
was Jackson, and that he was brother to the

one who shot Col. Ellsworth. Seeing that
Zouave lying there helpless and dead, he
walked up to where he lay, took hold of his
hand, and, while he was looking at him, discovered a ring upon his finger. He instantly
recognized that ring. It was a ring given to
this Zouave by a beautiful girl in Alexandria,
as a parting gift. He no doubt had promised
to wear that ring as long as he lived, and he
had kept his word. Jackson had offered himself to the same girl, and had been refused.
Now was the time for revenge. Before he
could be stopped, he had severed that finger
from the hand; and, as he fled, he was heard
to say, "I will carry this ring back to the giver,
and tell her that I have had my revenge." I
was unarmed, and in one sense helpless; and
I am now glad that I was, for my hands are
not stained with that man's blood.

I will mention one other incident before I
leave the hospital, and I do it to show how
strongly a horse will sometimes become at-
tached to his master. An officer was brought
into the hospital, the next morning, in a dying
condition. His horse was also wounded, but

was standing beside his master when the officer was discovered. The horse followed them
to the hospital, and hung around all day. The
officer was buried, the next day, not far from
the hospital. The horse seemed to know that
it was his master whom they buried, for he
stayed by that grave as long as I stayed at the
hospital. I dressed his wound and did everything I could for the poor horse. It was
distressing to see that horse walking or paw-
ing, and occasionally neighing, around his
master's grave. What became of him I know
not.

On the 25th of July, I had the pleasure of
meeting Gen. Beauregard. He told me that
I was to go to Richmond with the rest of the
prisoners, and after the wounded recovered so
that they would not need my assistance, I
should be exchanged. But when that time
came, Gen. Beauregard was leading his army
on other battle fields; and I never saw or heard
from him, after I was placed under the control
of the most heartless men that the sun ever
shone upon.

I never shall forget our journey to Rich-

mond. The wounded suffered terribly. At
places where the train stopped, the wounded
would beg for water, but they were almost
always refused. They were insulted in every
conceivable way. The engineer would pull
the throttle out and start the train very suddenly, then reverse the steam and stop perfectly still, then start again, and continue
starting and stopping for a long time, on purpose to annoy those poor wounded men. All
the while, the crowd which had gathered about
the depot would be shouting, "Give it to them."

We at last arrived at Richmond. I had got
there sooner than I expected, when I left my
home, and I had arrived there under different
circumstances from what I had ever anticipated. We were huddled into a large brick
building, and a strong guard was placed around
us. We soon found out that the building had
been used for a tobacco factory. The most of
us could endure the strong smell of tobacco,
but before we got out, we found that the disa-
greeable scent of tobacco was a little part of
what we had to endure.

While at Richmond, I became intimately

acquainted with Michael Corcoran, colonel of
the 69th, and for months after had a good
chance to study his character. While at
Richmond, an occurrence took place which
proved very much to my disadvantage. A
number of the prisoners escaped from the
prison. Soon after, I was summoned to appear
before the body of men who, it seemed, had
charge of the prison. I was questioned concerning those men who had escaped. I was
asked, among other questions, if I knew that
those men were calculating to escape. I told
them that I did know that they intended to
make the attempt. They asked me why I did
not inform them of the fact. My answer dis-
pleased them very much, and I could plainly
see that my doom was sealed. By some means
or other, they had also taken a dislike to Col.
Corcoran. We always expressed our opinions
upon all subjects, when asked, but time proved
that we had to suffer on account of our honest
opinions.

We were soon sent to Charleston jail.
Charleston is situated on a tongue of land
formed by the junction of Cooper and Ashley

rivers, which communicate with the ocean seven miles below. The plan of the city is regular, its streets crossing each other at right angles. The harbor is guarded by Fort Sumter, at the entrance. Fort Sumter stands on a little island, about four miles from the city. Fort Moultrie and Castle Pinckney also guard the city. The journey from Richmond to Charleston was a dreary one. If I am any judge, the country is very poor in many respects. The negroes lived in huts; and their masters lived in houses, which were set upon posts five or six feet from the ground. In many places the hogsty was underneath the house. When we arrived at the jail, we were received by the jailer, and conducted to our cells.

We arrived in Charleston soon after the North had taken a crew who called themselves privateers. The North called them pirates. We expected that the North would hang every one of them, and expressed ourselves accordingly. We were not long in our new quarters before we were called upon by some of the dignitaries of Charleston. At first, they

seemed pleased to form our acquaintance, and
said that they would do all they could to make
our visit pleasant.   Very soon, one of the party
went to a window, and called our attention to
an object which was in the prison yard.   On
looking out, we saw the same number of ropes
suspended, with loops at the ends, that there
were of the pirates which the North had just
taken.   Turning to us, with a leer such as none
but a Southerner can express, he said, "Gentlemen, if your Northern friends hang those
privateers, just so many of you will hang
there."   Col. Corcoran straightened himself
up, and, with defiance flashing in his eyes, made
this reply: "We all realize that we are in your
power, at present, and we know that you can
do with us as you please.   It is the duty of the
North to hang those men, and I hope that they
will not shirk their duty."   And many of the
prisoners said, "Amen!"   Those brazen faced
men soon left the cell, and we saw them no
more.

While at Richmond, we had food enough,
such as it was, but now it was very scant.   The
prison was very filthy, and well stocked with

vermin. Our sufferings were intensified. We now disposed of everything of any value which we had, except the dirty clothes which we had on our backs, to procure food and medicine. "What will come next?" was the question often asked, but seldom answered. Still we were hopeful.

The jail was a large brick building on Broad street. We were confined in an upper room, the windows of which were barred, and closed with iron shutters, except one very small one, overlooking a very narrow street in the rear of the building. One night we heard the cry of "Fire! Fire!" and our prison cell, for the first time since we arrived, was illuminated. As nearly as we could judge, the fire broke out in a gas house, next door to a sash and blind factory. The fire spread with great rapidity. Great efforts were made to extinguish it, without the slightest effect. The engines, worked by negroes, seemed utterly powerless, and the flames spread, finally, to the jail. The roof soon took fire. No movement was made to let the prisoners out. We could hear the guards making the doors more secure. At first we

were not alarmed, for we expected, in case the
fire should reach the jail, we should be let out;
but when we heard the cry, "The jail is on
fire!" and heard the guards making the door
more secure, we were dismayed. At that time
our room was so filled with smoke that we
expected very soon to be suffocated. We
formed ourselves into a circle and commenced
marching around, and as we passed by the
window we would take a breath and then pass
on. The heat was becoming intense; but at
last the fire was subdued and we were saved,
for what purpose we knew not. At this time
our allowance of food was one pint of oatmeal
and one quart of stagnant water a day.

Soon after the fire, we were removed to
Castle Pinckney, where our sufferings were
beyond description. [The author would attempt to give a partial description, but he
knows that some of the doctor's relatives would
say, "Please forbear."]

After a while, we were removed from Castle
Pinckney to Columbia. Columbia is pleasantly
situated near the center of the state, at the
confluence of Broad and Saluda rivers, which,

when united, form the Congaree. I think that
the rebels were afraid that we might be rescued,
was why they removed us to an inland prison.

You would be surprised to know how much,
news we gathered while we were in those prisons. Our eyes and ears were constantly
open, and we were constantly on the alert.
We caught every sound within our hearing,
and everything which passed within our vision
was thoroughly scanned. We gathered a
great deal of information by hearing the boys
and negroes talking in the streets.

One more incident I must not omit concerning our prospects while we were in Charleston.
One morning, while we were in Charleston
jail, an old man made his appearance at the prison, and asked permission to see Col. Corcoran.
At first he was refused, but after a consultation
with the prison officials, he was admitted. He
was a man of medium height, with gray hair,
and large dark eyes. His general appearance
denoted that he was no ordinary man. What
his business was with Col. Corcoran, we could
not conjecture. They had an interview in one
corner of our cell, and we could see by the

colonel's manner, that this man was not an
enemy. After his departure, Col. Corcoran,
with tears glistening in his eyes, turned to us
and said, "Comrades, we have a friend who
has power to enter our cell." And we all, as
if in concert, said, "Bless the Lord!" He was
a Catholic priest of high standing. He followed
us to Columbia, and through him the colonel
obtained money, medicine, and clothing. If it
had not been for that old priest, we could not
have lived. After we left Columbia, we saw
him no more. God bless that old man! He
will receive his reward after he has passed
through the pearly gates of heaven.

Our suffering, while at Columbia, was not so
great as it was at Charleston. We had more
and better food, and the prison officials seemed
to be a little more humane. By catching a
word here and a word there, we kept better
posted than any one would think it possible
for us to do. Nothing transpired while we
were at Columbia worth relating. It was
about the same old prison life.

We were removed from Columbia back to
Richmond. This was in the spring of 1862.

I found Richmond prison about the same as when I left it, only more filthy. From what we could learn, we concluded that the North was still hopeful, and determined to put down the rebellion, at whatever sacrifice it might cost. At that time I was very much broken down.

I was removed from Richmond to Salisbury. At that prison the prisoners suffered fearfully. Food was very scarce, and disease was sending many of the prisoners out of hearing of the clamor of men. The prisoners at Salisbury were confined in an open lot, or more strictly speaking, in an open pen. This pen was surrounded by a board fence, and the prisoners were guarded by men of the lowest type of humanity. The poor prisoners did not need much guarding, for most of them were so feeble and emaciated that they could not have escaped if they could have had a chance. They were exposed to all kinds of weather, most of them without shelter of any kind. Many dug holes to crawl into to protect themselves from the scorching sun in summer, or the cold storms in winter. Food and

water were of the poorest kind. All the water
they had was taken from a sluggish pool
which was in one corner of the pen, mingled
with all kinds of filth, and surrounded with the
miasma of death. Oh, that prison pen at Salisbury! We not only had to endure the famine and the fever, but the fiendish looking
eyes of those rebels glared at us. Such is a
passing glimpse of the prison yard at Salisbury.

At this time all hopes of ever seeing my
friends or home again had almost vanished. I
had not heard one word from my wife or any
of my friends, since I was taken prisoner. I
knew that my friends would do all that mortal
friends could do for me. I also knew that my
wife would be almost insane, and that my poor
old father and mother would suffer terribly on
account of my being where they could not
know how I was faring, but I was glad they
could not. I knew that all avenues through
which my friends could reach me, were securely
closed. I was sure that I could not live much
longer under such treatment. Despondency
was strongly affecting my mind. I would turn

my mind homeward, and hope that the foundation of our national power still stood strong.
I had great confidence in the ability of our
government, and I felt assured that, sooner or
later, rebellion would be put down. Often, on
bended knees, I would ask God to save our
country, and to spare my life until rebellion
was wiped from our land.

At last, I was taken from the prison pen at
Salisbury, and left upon the banks of the James
river, completely destitute. For what purpose
I was left there, in that condition, I can assign
but one reason, and that is that they left me
there to die. I took a survey of my situation,
and while doing so, these words flashed
through my mind; "Hope on, hope ever." I
was without food, and my wardrobe I will not
attempt to describe. I had often read about
Elijah being fed by the ravens. Would they
feed me? Just as the sun was sinking behind
the western hills, I discovered an old negro
stealthily approaching me. Was he friend or
foe? That was the question which ran through
my mind. As he came near, I discovered that
he had a basket in his hand, and that he was

constantly scanning the country in every direction, as if he was about to do something which he wished to keep secret. Just before he got to where I was standing, he stopped, and looked in every direction. After convincing himself that there was no one in sight of us, he approached me. Setting the basket down, he said, "This will keep mas'r alive; best I got." He turned and was soon out of sight. The raven had come. The basket contained what those negroes call hoe cakes. I ate a good supper, and laid myself down to rest. I slept the best that night I had for months. The next morning I felt refreshed. Everything was still, and that was something new to me. The food seemed to strengthen me. I felt like a new man. The next day, my mind was occupied with different plans concerning how I should cross the river; but before my plans were consummated, I discovered a steamer coming up the river. It was coming very slowly, and to all appearance was out reconnoitering. I could see that the men were scanning the banks of the river. I was soon convinced that it was a Northern steamer.

The following lines had been running through my mind all that day.

> Lead, kindly Light, amid the encircling gloom,
> Lead Thou me on!
> The night is dark, and I am far from home;
> Lead Thou me on!
>
> Keep Thou my feet! I do not care to see
> The former scenes; O banish them from me!

As the steamer slowly moved up the river, something seemed to say, "Now is the time for you to make an exertion." I at once began to do everything which I could to attract their attention. Soon I was overjoyed to see the steamer stop. I could see that they were lowering a boat, and soon I saw them pulling for the shore. At first they thought that I was placed there as a decoy to entrap them; but after the captain had viewed me through his glass, he thought otherwise, and ordered his men to come and see what I wanted. I told those men that I had been a prisoner a long time, and wished to get once more within the Union lines. They took me to the steamer, and I once more stood beneath our starry banner, FREE.

I had come out of those loathsome prisons
as people generally do who are imprisoned for
conscience' sake, more devoted than ever to the
cause for which I suffered. I was kindly
received by all on board of the steamer, and
everything done for me which could be done
to make me comfortable. The captain, seeing
my feeble condition, ordered all the officers
and crew not to annoy me by asking questions.
I told the captain my name, and that I was
surgeon of the third Connecticut regiment.
He told me that he had often heard me spoken
of by many noted men. My filthy wardrobe
was exchanged for one more comfortable and
better adapted to my station. My hair was
cut and I was thoroughly shampooed, and ere
long I was on my way to Washington.

As soon as I arrived in Washington, I was
taken to a hotel and had a long interview with
many of the dignitaries. Afterward I had an
interview with the President and Secretary
Stanton. At that time all the reliable information which could be gathered concerning the
rebels' movements, was highly prized. I was

constantly surrounded by reporters, but after
I had given the President and Secretary Stanton all the information which I could concerning the South, I closed the doors upon the
reporters. The newspaper men and the telegraph companies were posting their patrons
with all the news which they could glean from
every source. It was not strange that the
people were anxious to learn all they could
concerning the war, for there was hardly a
family but what had relatives in our army.
Still it was very important to keep some of the
information which was procured by our leading
men concerning the rebels' movements out of
the papers, for the rebels would, in spite of all
we could do, get hold of our newspapers and
be much benefited.

Long before I reached Washington, the
particulars of my escape were published in the
papers and the telegraph wires had carried
them to the remotest parts of the North. My
friends at Thompson and other places had
heard the vibrations as the wires carried the
glad tidings with lightning speed throughout
the country.

As soon as Col. Corcoran heard that the
doctor was once more in the land of the free,
he hastened to meet him. They met at
Washington, and such a meeting is not often
seen. When first they met, they clasped hands
and with bowed heads offered up thanks to
God for their deliverance. For a long time
neither could speak. Probably the trials and
sufferings which they had endured together
while in those Southern prisons, flashed
through their minds. One of the party who
came on with Col. Corcoran to escort the doctor to New York, said, "I have seen Corcoran
when the chances for his life were not one
in ten thousand, and where the earth was
strewn with the dead and dying, but I never
saw him affected as he was at that meeting."
Corcoran and his party did everything in their
power to make the journey from Washington
to New York pleasant for the doctor.

His stay in New York was very short, for
he was very anxious to meet the loved ones at
home. As he neared his home, no doubt his
heart swelled with emotion, for there would be

a scene as trying to the nerves as any which
he had passed through. It was his wish to
return in a very quiet manner. He delayed
his coming on purpose to take his friends by
surprise. They expected him in the morning,
but he did not come until evening. They were
not disposed to have him surprise them in his
coming. When he arrived at Thompson depot,
a carriage stood waiting to take him to his
home. As they drove from the depot, he
thought his wish was to be granted. It was
evening and quite dark. He had questioned
the driver on many points, but the driver
seemed disposed not to be very talkative.
Afterward he learned the reason why the
driver was so mute. As he entered the village, the bells in the steeples commenced
ringing out the glad tidings, and at the same
moment many familiar voices broke the stillness of the evening by singing one of his
favorite hymns, "Home again, home again."
He then discovered that he was surrounded by
the village people, who had turned out in a
mass to receive him. He was then escorted
to his home, the multitude dispersed in a quiet

manner, and he was left to enjoy once more the presence of his family friends. He arrived home on Saturday evening, August 3d, 1862. The next day he escorted to church, to all appearance, one of the happiest women on earth. The scene at the church after the services were closed, can better be imagined than described. The congregation encircled him, and all were eager to press his hand once more. For days his home was thronged with friends from far and near, all anxious to hear him relate his experience while he was in those Southern prisons.

At times he was almost afraid that he would become demented. His experience in the fourteen months seemed more like a horrid dream than a reality; but as time passed on, his flesh and strength returned, his mind became more clear, and he was ready to go at them again. He could not endure the hardships of an army life, but he thought that he could yet do something for his country.

At this time the government was holding out great inducements to volunteers. It was reported that many of the negroes at the South

would volunteer if they could get to the North.
Col. Nichols and the doctor concluded to go
to New York, charter a steamer, take on board
what provisions they thought would be necessary to supply the number of men which they
calculated to bring from the South, and go
to Hilton Head and try their luck, thinking
that by so doing they might aid and assist our
government. They carried out their contem-
plated plans to the letter, except the main
point; they did not get the men. Unforeseen
orders passed by the government soon after
they left New York, were the cause of their
failure to get the men. A full description of
that voyage would be interesting to some, but
I will mention only one incident, and then
pass on.

On the second day after leaving Hilton
Head, the captain discovered a ship which
acted rather strangely. As it came nearer,
he also discovered that it was armed to the
teeth. He at once ordered the engineer to
make the best time which it was possible for
him to do with safety. For four hours the two
vessels tried their skill in fast running. They

could see that the vessel was slowly gaining upon them. Soon a Northern ship was seen ahead of them. It proved to be an armed ship, and a ship was never seen to change its course quicker than the one that was chasing them. The captain said that he had no doubt it was a privateer.

They landed at New York all safe and sound, but terribly disappointed. The doctor had been disappointed so many times that it did not affect him as much as it would some others. One object which they had in going after those negroes, was to avoid a draft which would be levied upon Connecticut unless the quota was raised by men volunteering.

What had his friends been doing all the time while he was a prisoner? They had been doing everything in their power for his benefit, but all their doings were of no avail. Every avenue through which they thought he could be reached was thoroughly closed. His wife and sister went to Washington and had an interview with President Lincoln and Secretary Stanton concerning what course to take to have him released if he was alive. Stanton

told them that there was but one course for
them to pursue, and that was by exchange.
They were willing to do any and everything
which could be done for his release, or for his
comfort. They gave his wife a writing author-
izing her to select any one of the rebel officers
which the North held as prisoners of war, and
for her to take any course to accomplish an
exchange. The rebels were approached in
many ways, but to no purpose. They would
not release him under any circumstances.

Dr. Hosford, an eminent physician, supplied
his place as physician and surgeon while he
was away; and as his health would not admit
of his resuming his former practice after he
returned, he was at liberty to do whatever little thing he could for his country. He spoke
in many different places, describing his tour at
the South while he was a prisoner in the rebels'
hands, and urging our young men to stand
firm for our country and to do whatever duty
presented itself to them.

This narrative relative to his war record is
in substance a true narrative, for I had it from
his own lips. A great many other interesting

things might be spoken of, but for fear of wearying the reader, I will cease writing about the war and let the curtain drop to shut from our view those terrible scenes which the war produced.

This life is something like the seasons of the year. To give a relish to this life we have Spring and Autumn, Summer and Winter. It is our adversities which make the pleasures of this life enjoyable. We must have Winter to enjoy Spring. Spring would be but dreary weather if we had nothing else but Spring.

I think that I am safe in saying that at this time he had a large number of warm and influential friends. After he had somewhat recovered his health, his friends in Windham County selected him for their senator to represent them in the State Legislature. He told his friends that it would be placing him out of his sphere, and as he had no desire for the position, he would rather not accept. His friends argued that he was their choice, and hoped that he would not go contrary to their unanimous wish. After consulting upon the matter he accepted, and I think that his friends

had just cause to be proud of their senator.
He was appointed as chairman on some of the
most important committees, and his acts gave
general satisfaction. His sayings and doings
while he was senator, gained him a reputation
which any man should prize very highly. He
did not desire to be in office, for that would
place him out of his sphere. Surgery was his
whole aim, and he could not be contented
in doing anything else. Being so long in
those Southern prisons had weakened his constitution and made terrible inroads upon his
general health, so much so that he could not
endure the long rides over the hilly country
which surrounds Thompson. Consequently,
he was obliged to seek a place where his
practice would be confined to a smaller sphere.
Providence had just lost her most noted
surgeon. Dr. Miller had passed from earth,
and Rhode Island mourned the loss.

In July, 1865, Dr. McGregor moved to
Providence, took rooms at the City Hotel, and
opened an office at 51 Dorrance street. He
very soon commanded a large practice in his
profession. His reputation as surgeon and

physician was already established. He was now 44 years old. His practice was so extensive, and his success in his operations so great, that he did not propose to lay down the knife to any one in Rhode Island.

We can review the past and have some knowledge of the present, but we know not what the future has in store for us. When everything looks prosperous and bright, when the morning zephyr plays gently with the tiny flowers, and even when the midday sun shines in all its loveliness, we know not but a cyclone is forming beyond the hills, which, before evening, will destroy all our hopes and blast all our prospects. How many there are who will say this is true! "A calm is often followed by a storm," is the saying of mariners. When a useful man in the meridian of life, one who has always applied his talents in the right direction, is suddenly cut down, the whole country mourns the loss. The next scene, which I am rapidly approaching, was too tragical and heart-rending to admit of a minute description without lacerating the hearts of many, therefore I will give only some of the main facts and pass on to other scenes.

The eventful 4th of November, 1867, dawned upon the city of Providence in all its beauty. The bells chimed in harmony, and the reverberations sounded through the streets. All the forenoon the doctor had been going from one sick-room to another, administering to his patients. Noon came and he repaired to the City Hotel for dinner. Little did he think that it was to be his last meal on earth. His wife had left the city a few days previous to visit relatives and friends at Thompson. After dinner he again entered upon his duties. He was on his way to visit the Hon. Joseph M. Blake's daughter, who was very sick at that time. On driving down Dyer street, feeling perfectly safe, no doubt, the hind part of his chaise was struck by the cars, and he was thrown underneath and terribly mangled. He was immediately taken to his rooms at the City Hotel, and medical assistance summoned. It was found, on examination, that one of his arms was fearfully crushed, and that amputation would be necessary. He was put under the influence of ether, and the operation commenced. His pulse sank rapidly, and it was soon discovered that he would not survive the operation. When the last stroke of the knife was finished, and the arm severed from his body, it was found that the immortal part of Dr. McGregor had crossed the river of death. His sufferings, both physical and mental, in this life had been great, but he had borne them with Christian fortitude. Thus ended the life of Dr. John McGregor; and thus he passed from earth, leaving a name and memory which will never die.

When the news flashed over the country, describing that tragical scene on Dyer street and that terrible scene at the City Hotel, where the operation was performed, and the ending of his life, there was a solemn thrill throughout the land. The excitement in Providence, and especially at the Hotel, was intense. It seemed so strange that after he had been exposed to the many dangers of the battle field, and to the fever and the famine which enveloped those Southern prisons, and his life had been spared, he should be sacrificed in a city where people should be protected against such calamities. There are many things which happen to which our feeble minds cannot be reconciled; and that is one of the cases where some minds are still unreconciled. We believe that he is now at rest. We know that the clamor of war cannot reach his ears, and we know that the fever and famine will not have to be endured.

The scene at the Hotel, when Mrs. McGregor arrived and found that her husband was dead, I will not attempt to describe, for the English language is inadequate to describe such a heart-rending scene. For days the Hotel was thronged with sympathizing friends, all more than willing to aid and assist in any way which they could to alleviate the sorrow and suffering of the widow and relatives, and to watch over and prepare the dead for burial.

On the 10th, his remains were carefully removed from the City Hotel to the Beneficent Congregational Church, where Rev. James G. Vose preached the following discourse occasioned by the death of Dr. John McGregor.

DISCOURSE.

"*Duty amid Danger.*"

My days are swifter than a post: they flee away: they see no good. They are passed away as the swift ships: as the eagle that hasteth to the prey.

Job ix: 25.

This utterance of the patriarch has been impressed on my mind from early childhood. Something in the quaintness of phrase attracted my attention, and fixed the words upon my memory from the first hearing. In the whole poem there is a richness and variety of metaphor which strike the ear of the most careless, and haunt us like a strain of melody. In the lines before us, we have three figures to denote the shortness of life. The first is that of a rider, who bears tidings, and though the rapidity of our steam and telegraph lines seems to cast a satire upon the post riding, whatever it were, of that early age; yet the coming and departing of such a messenger is an apt symbol of the horseman. Death, who appears across the plains as a dim speck, and is upon us before we fairly descry his garments. "My days are swifter than a post, * * * they are passed away as the swift ships." Here also, the impression made upon the imagination is not so much of absolute speed, as of strange and unaccountable disappearance. The imagination is not affected by mere numbers. We know how fast light travels from the sun and from the fixed stars, but this does not impress us, as may some simple every day fact. He, who from some overlooking height, has gazed dreamily out on the ocean, on a still summer afternoon; and has seen a cluster of white winged ships, fresh freighted and trimmed for a foreign port, quietly dropping down the harbor, or steering their course out of the islands toward the unsheltered main,—he, who thus gazing has turned his eye for a moment to the heavens or to the distant city, or lost in thought, has forgotten, for a time, the objects before him, when he looks again, is startled to find that the ships have vanished, or perhaps he can just descry their masts sinking every moment below the horizon. Such an one, I say, will comprehend the figure of the sacred poet. "They are passed away as the swift ships." It is not the rapidity of their motion, but the suddenness of their disappearance that affects us. They may have seemed to loiter and almost be motionless, but the returning eye searches for them in vain. It sweeps the horizon o'er and o'er, but they are no more seen. "My days are swifter than a post: they are passed away as the swift ships; as the eagle that hasteth to the prey." The keen vision of the eagle, who looks with unblenched gaze at the sun, and his swift flight are facts well known. Here too we see that among a pastoral people the unlooked for attack upon their flocks would be a fit image of all sudden events. In all these figures, the idea is not of absolute swiftness, but of sudden and unexpected departure. Even so life passes. It may seem to linger, and often it is

wearisome. Job wished for the grave, and
longed to hide himself in its bosom; but looking at the past his days seemed to have vanished unawares.

The uncertainty of life is impressed upon us,
with every advancing month. Strange and
unlooked for events set at naught all our
planning, and give new truth to the Spanish
proverb, "Nothing is certain but the unforeseen." During the current year, in a general
condition of great health and quietness, we
have been called, in this city, to witness many
striking and sad events that have revived in
my thought continually the sublime imagery
of the sacred writer. "My days are swifter
than a post, they are passed away as the swift
ships."

I wish to draw no lesson of terror or dismay
from these sad events, but to lead you rather
to consider the claims of the present. My
theme is this, that *duty is not diminished by
uncertainty.*

I. There is a duty to guard against sickness and accident. I place duty to self first,
because it is God's claim. We may fulfil duty

to self without being selfish. We should love
ourselves, because God loves us. Many men
are deficient in self love. All the herd of
gluttons, drunkards, abusers of the body by
excess, are destitute of a right love of self.
They have no self-respect, no faith in their
high endowments or capacities, no sense of the
honor God has put on them, nor of the sacrifice Christ has made that they might be saved.
But others love themselves too little, who are
not contained in any such class as these. Men
and women there are, who throw away life for
money or for fashion, or for false appearances.
There are multitudes whose habits of life, of
dress, of daily employment are injurious to
health and fatal to long life. Many expose
themselves for amusement's sake, as others
with equal or even greater folly do it for gain.
Now it is no answer to all this to say, that we
cannot tell what will harm, or what will benefit
us, that we are liable to so many diseases and
troubles that we may as well disregard them
all. We know that there are certain laws of
temperance and regularity which cannot be
disregarded with impunity. We shall suffer

for their neglect. At all events we shall fall under the displeasure of God. If we had received from a friend a musical instrument of rare beauty and workmanship, and were told that it needed careful handling, that its strings would suffer from moisture and from sudden cold or heat, that it must not be shaken or jarred, or its notes struck violently or by an unskilled hand, we should certainly be very ungrateful and foolish to disregard these warnings. To be sure the fire may burn it, or some malicious or careless hand may destroy it, in spite of all our precautions, but shall we therefore neglect it altogether? We *have* received from God an instrument of more curious mechanism, than man can devise, and with good handling it may outlast most of the ordinary inventions of man. It may be continued to us seventy or eighty years. Because life is uncertain, because a thousand accidents and diseases surround us at all ages, shall we therefore neglect all bodily care and forethought?

You think perhaps this advice is needless. Men do take thought for their bodies. Many

of you are anxious and troubled on account of
some little ailment. You lie awake and are
restless with apprehension, because of some
slight pain, or some anticipated evil. You
hear of some disease that has affected a neighbor or caused his death, and you imagine it
may be that you have symptoms of the same,
and yet you yourself have been and are, perhaps, neglectful of the commonest rules of
bodily health. Neither your food, your sleep,
nor your exercise are guided by a sense of
duty to God. You forget that God will call
you to account for your body as well as for
your soul. You forget that in addition to the
pains and sickness brought on by wrong
doing, men will also have to answer for the
sin of abusing God's handiwork. Admit that
with our best precautions we cannot escape
suffering and danger, should we not the more
earnestly seek in all right ways to avoid all
needless harm and loss?

The same thing is true in reference to accident by the elements or the works of man. We
cannot stay the thunderbolt nor the earth-
quake, but we can avert the lightning from

our dwellings by the simple contrivance of Franklin. We can avoid needless danger. We can avoid reckless exposure. Yet how often is this duty forgotten! Men build railroads and run them without regard for human life. Through the streets of a populous city, or on even grade, across a travelled road, it makes little difference where, if there is money to be made. Traffic takes little note of life or limb. And there is too much indifference to the fearful anguish that may result from some false or unexpected movement. The iron wheels that bear such prodigious weight, may now and then go over a human heart, and crush the life out from other kindred hearts; and what amount of money, or business accommodation put into the opposite scale will balance that loss and anguish? The uncertainties of life relieve us from no caution public or private—they rather increase and force upon us the duty, both for ourselves and others, of obeying the rules of prudence, of temperance, of care, and circumspection, that we may not throw away the life which God has bestowed. Is it not a plain duty of all good governments and good citizens to see to it, that the lives of our fellowmen are not endangered by steam engines, and factories erected in dangerous places, by explosions in crowded streets,—by yielding to traffic and convenience all the claims that belong to the sacredness of life? Rhode Island has abolished capital punishment. She is too tender hearted to put to death even the worst of criminals. Shall we not make better laws for the safety of our citizens, as they walk or ride along our streets at midday? Is it not a solemn duty to secure our friends and our children, by all possible means, from such sad catastrophies? Of the numerous inventions of the present day to facilitate trade, or to improve the style and comfort of living, almost every one tends also to endanger or to shorten life; and we need the greatest care, by public laws, and by private efforts to defend ourselves and others from harm. It is the boast of our age, that human life is regarded as more sacred than it ever was before. And yet the most inhuman butcheries occur on railroads and steamboats, and within our cities almost every week, and are passed over as blameless accidents. God will call us to account, as men and citizens, for the recklessness and indifference that suffer so many precious lives to be destroyed.

II. And now I come, secondly, to a very different point presented by this theme, viz: That it is our duty to encounter dangers joyfully, when a real good is to be gained. Duty remains amid uncertainty. And when there is a substantial good to be gained, or when there is a fair hope of attaining it, we may rightly encounter danger. Men must encounter danger in the ordinary pursuits of business. They must travel over land and sea. They must run the risks of fire, of machinery, of the various tools and implements which they have in use. While these risks ought to be under far more strict regulation, they still must be bravely met. If men accept the industries which God sets before them, in a God-fearing manner, they have a right to trust his protection. If they are not carried away by love of gold, or fool-hardiness, then they may regard danger as encountered in obedience to Him.

And in many cases in life, God does plainly command us to advance in the very face of danger. We are called to expose ourselves for the sake of our friends and children. To save their lives we must willingly risk our own. Nay, sometimes for strangers or enemies, even, we ought to encounter peril to relieve them. No true hearted man will see the sick or wounded suffer and die, when he can afford them help, although the furnishing of that help may incur the danger of disease to himself. When a contagious disease breaks out in city or country, some friend must minister to the sufferer. There is responsibility somewhere to furnish aid and nursing and medical skill. There is a duty higher than that of self-preservation. And this is recognized, thank God! Human nature, corrupt and imperfect as it is, still recognizes the duty of mutual help. And many a timid woman, and many a generous boy, and many a poor sailor, even, will forget all thought of self, and spring to the side of the suffering, when there is the least hope of rescuing or comforting them in their distress.

At times, it is the highest duty to forget all fear. Nay, at times it is the highest safety, also. For, in cities, where the pestilence has raged, or where the yellow fever has swept off thousands, it is found that those who have been most generous and sympathizing,—the faithful physician, the attentive nurse, the sister of mercy,—have been protected of God through all dangers, while the cowering fugitive, or the selfish neglecter of the suffering, has fallen a victim. It is God's command that we live in this world for high objects, and that these should always rise above mere personal safety or comfort. This does not conflict with the claims of our own body and soul, for the chief motive why these should be supported, is that they may be useful in God's sight. It is not easy to draw any distinct line for all cases, but he who studies the character of Christ and the example of all noble, useful men in the world, will learn how to fulfill duty to self and duty to others, at the same time.

In the breaking out of our war, our young men learned this lesson—I think I may say all classes of society learned it. Men and

women, young and old; all professions and all
ages, learned it. None more certainly than
our physicians, who offered themselves read-
ily to care for the sick and wounded, and to
go with them to prison or to death. And thus
it is sometimes, in life,—the greater the danger, the greater the duty. If it be a plain
duty, if God commands, and love and honor
light the way, then danger and peril only
increase the obligation, as they increase the
honor.

III. I come, therefore, thirdly, to remark
that amid all the uncertainties of this life, it is
still our duty to remember the obligations due
to the present. We possess only the present.
Our sphere of action, our power of control
upon ourselves and others is limited. The
good act will, indeed sweep onward in waves of
influence, but the pebble we cast must be cast
into the present, if at all. The question for us
is not what shall be on the morrow, not where
we shall be, nor where shall be our neighbor or
child, but what we may do to-day, to comfort
and bless them. We need a more child-like
spirit, that we may thank God for the gifts of

the present, that we may enjoy them tranquilly, and impart them with a child's sweetness to others. The present comfort and health of our household and those committed to our care, involve ample duties, which must for the greater part of the time engross us. It is of vast importance that we live lives of kindness, of tenderness and self-denial, that we make home happy by the radiance of a cheerful and contented spirit. Grief and trouble will come soon enough. Let us not cloud the present sunshine, let us not fret and repine because of coming ill. Terrible events are about us; let us yield them the tear of sympathy, but let us not be too much cast down. For God calls us to make others happy and to point their eyes to the spot of sunshine on the distant hills. A life of gentle faith, of silent endurance, is pleasing in the sight of God. What though the darkness lowers, the gracious God is behind it. I have heard aged people describe the dark day, which occurred in 1780. The darkness was so great, that all ordinary business was suspended. The cattle came home from the pasture; the fowls sought their

nightly perch; lamps were lighted at midday,
and men's faces wore the look of terror and
dismay. At that time the Connecticut Assembly was sitting, and some proposed that they
should adjourn, for the day of judgment was
coming; but one of the members, stern old
Abraham Davenport, declared that, if the end
of the world were come, they could be found
in no better place than at their post of duty.
And Whittier describes him in his fine lines,
as saying —

This well may be the day of judgment which the world awaits.
But be it so or not, I only know
My present duty, and my Lord's command
    To occupy till he come.
And therefore with all reverence will I say.
Let God do His work, we will see to ours.

Thus should we remember, friends, our obligations to the present. God has set us in our
post of duty to live humbly, patiently and lov-
ingly, remembering the happiness of all who
are about us. There has always been, to my
mind, a strong *a priori* argument against those
who attempt to show from prophecy when the
end of the world will be, that the whole spirit

of the Bible commands us to fulfill present
duty. And it would be contrary to the whole
spirit of faith and duty, that God should reveal
the future. "Secret things belong unto the
Lord our God, but those which are revealed
belong unto us and to our children, that we
may do the works of this law." We must
remember, then, our obligations to the present.
It is well to live by the day, not laying too
many plans for this life, not over confident of
anything concerning it, but anxious that the
present time be well and wisely employed.

Men sometimes say, in hollow phrase, that
we ought to live each day as if it were the last.
Such a life would be miserable and useless. If
you knew this to be your last day, you would
spend it in farewells to your friends, and in
closing up the business of life. But you do
not know it to be your last day. What then?
Let us use it wisely. Be sure it will be the
last day to some. In this city one thousand
persons die a year, an average of three a day.
Very rarely does a day pass but it is the last
for some one, who had found a home here.
They die by accident or disease, by many

dreaded or undreaded ways. It will do us no harm to think of it sometimes,—"To smell to a fresh turf," says Thomas Fuller, "is wholesome to the body,—even so the thoughts of mortality are healthful to the soul." How, then, shall I use this thought? I will be kindly, humble, true to every man I meet in business or social life. I will be gentle and patient in the house and in the shop. I will make life easier and better for friends and children. Above all, I will be true to the soul's need, and remember that to-day is all we are sure of to prepare for heaven. I will, therefore, take all fitting times to impress religious truth upon the souls of men, that, if that strange lot which is cast every day for one or more of the dwellers of this city, should fall among my family, or within my circle of influence, I may rejoice that the duty of the day has been well done. It is not for me to forebode disaster or trouble, but to leave all in the hands of God, who will cause all things to work together for good to those that love Him. The simplicity of such a life is well expressed in a German hymn, which I love to remember:

My God, I know not *when* I die,
What is the moment, or the hour,
How soon the clay may broken lie.
How quickly pass away the flower:
Then may thy child prepared be
Thro' time to meet eternity.

My God, I know not *how* I die,
For death has many ways to come.
In dark, mysterious agony.
Or gently as a sleep, to some.
Just as thou wilt. if but I be
Forever blessed, Lord, with Thee.

My God, I know not *where* I die,
Where is my grave, beneath what strand.
Yet, from its gloom, I do rely
To be delivered by thy hand.
Content I take what spot is mine,
Since all the earth, my Lord, is Thine.

My gracious God, when I must die,
Oh! bear my happy soul above,
With Christ, my Lord, eternally
To share thy glory and thy love!
Then comes it right and well to me,
When, where and how my death shall be.

Sudden deaths, dear friends, have multiplied among us of late. Among public and private

men, these strange and shocking events have
been of frequent occurrence. Such events
sound strangely amid the excitements and
business of this present life. In the strife of
elections, in the whirl of traffic and of pleasure,
the coming of death terrifies us, like a peal of
thunder. God doubtless sends these shocks
to startle men in their selfishness, and to teach
them the vanity of earthly things. But this is
but part of the lesson. It is not to hinder
the proper pursuits of life, it is not to paralyze
the arm that is uplifted in manly struggle. It
is rather to urge men to fulfill every duty as in
the sight of God. It is to press upon them the
sacredness of life, and the worth of every
moment. Great duties and small must be
attended to now, or else forever abandoned.
"Whatsoever thy hand findeth to do, do it
with thy might, for there is no work, nor
device, nor knowledge, nor wisdom, in the
grave whither thou goest." Too late, then, to
seek the forgiveness of God, too late to seek
the forgiveness of man, too late, also, to for-
give, if we have cherished animosities, or to
speak the word of tenderness and love, where

we have offended. Too late to recall the harsh and bitter speech, too late to do the act of self-denial for friends or children, or to bestow the gifts of charity on the starving or distressed. "He that is faithful, in that which is least, is faithful also in much." There is a prayer in the liturgy to be delivered from sudden death. I am told that in Newman Hall's chapel in London, where the liturgy is used in modified form, that prayer is rendered, "From sudden and unprepared death, Good Lord, deliver us." I take it this is the meaning of the prayer, and well for us, however and whenever death comes, if only we be found ready.

And now I will say a word in respect to the sad death of one of our own congregation, which has deeply affected this community. He has disappeared from our sight as in a moment. As a plummet sinks in the mighty waters, so has he vanished from our view in the ocean of eternity. Last Sabbath, in all the vigor of manly strength, with the hope of years of active labor and usefulness before him;— to-day, sleeping in his narrow bed. Dr. John

McGregor was born in Coventry, R. I. After his early education, he engaged in teaching school for a time, before entering upon his professional career. It was here, while just deciding upon the course of his future life, that his religious impressions became fixed and positive. Thoughtfully and with full purpose of heart, he gave himself to the Lord Jesus Christ. We have delightful evidence of the power of this change in the testimony of our own Sabbath School Superintendent, who was at that time his pupil. When the youthful teacher became a Christian, he deemed it his plain duty to inform his scholars of his new found faith, and not quailing before a trial which has often been found harder than to face the perils of battle, he summoned them around him, to begin their daily studies with prayer to God. His Christian character, borne witness to by those who have known him through a long life, was ever of this faithful type. He was a man of simple integrity, a man who never thought of turning aside from duty, however difficult.

As a professional man, there is abundant

and distinct evidence of his high attainments and success. In the State of Connecticut and in the county of Windham, where he resided he became well and favorably known, at a very early period in his practice. He was specially distinguished as a surgeon, and some remarkable cases, in which he was called, bear witness alike to his skill and his fidelity. Some of these have record in the scientific journals, and others are fondly cherished in the memory of grateful and admiring friends. A long account was given me last winter by a friend, of an extraordinary case of surgery performed by him, not only with marvelous skill and success, but with a fidelity and tenderness, wholly untainted by hope of reward.

And here let me bear witness, in honor of a profession for which I have the profoundest respect, that it does include, and has ever included, some of the most self-denying, most honorable and high minded men, that the world has ever seen. Among its ranks, there is less of sordidness, and far more of kindly, generous feeling, than in the ordinary walks of life. Of course there are painful exceptions. But I

speak now of what seems to be the tendency
and influence of this ennobling profession.
"Able, cautious and experienced physicians,"
says Martin Luther, "are the gifts of God.
They are the ministers of nature, to whom
human life is confided. No physician should
take a single step, but in humility and the fear
of God; they who are without the fear of God,
are mere homicides."

Dr. McGregor was an example, worthy of
his class. He never refused the cry of pov-
erty, nor ministered with any the less care or
assiduity in the homes of the poor and friend-
less. Blessed with a strong body and a tran-
quil mind, he was well endowed by nature for
his arduous task, and in the early part of his
life, when in full health, he traveled far and
near, in his country district, to attend upon
the suffering. There are many living to-day
who remember with gratitude his faithful
attentions. Some whose lives were saved, and
others whose troubles were cured or assuaged,
will learn with sincere sorrow of his painful
death.

Truly are fulfilled in him the sweet words of

the poet.

> " How many a poor man's blessing went
> With him beneath the low green tent,
> Whose curtain never outward swings!"

Of his military career, I cannot speak at great length, nor is there any need. The main facts are too impressive to demand the addition of details. With the breaking out of the rebellion, he deemed it his duty to offer his services to the government. He regarded his skill and experience as justly claimed by his countrymen, and he went out in one of the earliest regiments, which went forward to the conflict. It was the third Conn. Vol., a three months regiment, but not for him a three months campaign. In the disastrous battle of Bull Run, which fell like a crushing weight on every true freeman's heart, our friend was taken prisoner. It is distinctly testified, that this was owing to his firm determination not to forsake his men. He knew that none would care for the sick and wounded as he could do it, and he would not leave them, and therefore he went voluntarily to an imprisonment, which was worse than death. From prison to prison he followed his suffering comrades, until so emaciated that his manly frame was reduced to half its usual weight. Dear friends, these scenes must not be dwelt on. They are too bitter and too painful.

After remaining on the battle field seventeen days; on any one of which he might have escaped, had he been willing to desert his sick and dying comrades; he was taken to Richmond, and thence after a short time removed to Castle Pinckney. Afterwards he was removed to Charleston Jail, where he suffered incredible anguish from sickness and privation. During this time a great fire occurred, and the walls of the prison were heated through and its dark cells lighted up by the flame. The poor prisoners locked in and guarded as they were, viewed death inevitable. But the conflagration was stayed, and our friend who had endured such tortures of mind and body, was carried to Columbia, to Salisbury, and again to Richmond, from whence he was at length released. In these thirteen months of his captivity, he saw and felt as much of the

agony and cruelty of our civil war, as any man
perhaps could be able to see and live.

But it is sweet to think, that this faithful
surgeon comforted so many of the suffering,
saved the lives and relieved the distresses of
so many.

This was his reward, this the joy and solace
of his personal sacrifices. In looking back
upon these anguished days, he never regretted
the course he had taken, nor esteemed it other
than an honor and a privilege, that he was
counted worthy to suffer in so great a cause.
No man ever heard a boastful narrative from
him of these troubled days, nor would his natural modesty suffer any but a little circle of
familiar friends to draw from him the history
of his army life. Many who met him on our
streets or received him into their houses, had
little thought that he deserved a place high on
the roll of those who were ready to give life,
and more than life for the salvation of their
country.

We claim him to-day as our brother in this
church, for although his name is not on our
list, yet he had expressed his intention of uni-

ting with us, and I hold in my possesion the letter which he brought from the church, in his former home, cordially commending him, to us, as a brother faithful and beloved.

As it was beautifully said, at our prayer meeting last Tuesday evening, the hands of this church fellowship were soon to have been raised in welcome to this newly admitted member. But already the hands of angels and the spirits of the just have wafted him a sweeter and a purer welcome, to the church of the first born, whose names are written in heaven.

It was, indeed, a most sad and melancholy catastrophe, by which he was snatched away from earth. I wish not at this time, to make any harsh or criminating charges against individuals, but certainly there is blame somewhere. The life that God had spared through such terrible cruelties, and amid all the perils of war,—ought not to have been poured out on the altar of traffic, ought not to have been destroyed by a miserable system of railroad management. May it be a warning that may lead to better and safer ways of answering the claims of business, and providing for the transportation of goods. "I can create a thousand noblemen, in a day," said the king of France, "but I cannot make one philosopher." So may we say in our age,—we can make and transport innumerable bales of merchandise, but we cannot restore the life of a noble citizen, which is worth them all. No wonder that the desolate and bereaved heart cannot look, save with uncontrolled anguish, upon so dreadful an event. It is not in human nature to regard it calmly. And if the spirit rises against the thought, as if unwilling to admit it, I know there is love and patience in the heart of God. I remember that when our Divine Master met the weeping Mary at Bethany, and she reproached him, saying—"Lord, if thou hadst been here, my brother had not died,"—he made no answer, but only groaned in spirit. Such is the sympathy, even now, which Jesus has for every suffering soul.

But let us turn our eyes to the glorious record of the faithful. Let us behold this noble martyr crowned among those who have served God faithfully to the end. It was not ordered of a wise Providence that he should

die amid the many perils of the war. He
escaped them almost as by a miracle. The
shield of the Almighty was over him, in the
day of conflict. His spirit went not up in the
shout and smoke of battle. Nor did he die
with those who sank away in the hospital or
in the stockade. What a mockery upon
human foresight, do the circumstances of his
death afford us! Here, in our peaceful city,
pursuing the rounds of his benign art, he
meets the death, which seemed unable to find
him when clothed with all the panoply of war.

He was separated for a little time from those
brave heroes, whom he nursed and comforted
in their dying hours. But he is none the less
a martyr in the cause of humanity. And in
the records of heaven, his name will be treas-
ured among those who have sacrificed their all
for their nation and for God.

SERVICES AT PHENIX.

After the services at the church were over, the funeral train left Providence for Phenix. At Phenix, the people received his remains as their own. They said, "He comes back to us, his work finished." It was the desire of Mr. William C. Ames and family that the remains of Dr. McGregor should be taken to his house, and there rest until the next day, when there would be services at the Methodist Episcopal Church, previous to burial.

On November 11th, Rev. Mr. Westgate, assisted by Rev. Mr. Tallman of Thompson and Rev. Mr. Shepard, preached a very instructive discourse. After the services, his remains were removed to the tomb at Greenwood Cemetery. At last, the earthly journey was over. There, surrounded by his weeping relatives and friends, he was carefully laid away to sleep, after his work was done. And the widow followed her fond husband to his last earthly resting place, and, in his grave, buried her hopes of happiness here, and returned comfortless to her desolate home.

On a lofty eminence overlooking Phenix, and many other villages for miles around, stands a massive monument denoting the burial place of Dr. John McGregor. This monument will stand as long as the stars, like angels' eyes, through the clear sky so beautifully bright, look down upon this city of the dead; or the crescent moon sheds its pale light o'er these graves, as it sinks behind the western hills; or the first rays of the morning sun form the dew drops upon this monument into tears, and scatter them upon the grave beneath. It will stand until all the graves on the land, the catacombs of the east, and all the seas, are called upon to give up the dead. Then, and not until then, will the monuments of genius and the arts fall alike, and mingle with the fragments of fallen grandeur.

The knowledge of events, and the state of things in times past, have been communicated to us by inscriptions found upon visible monuments. Thus we find that when the Hebrews crossed the Jordan to invade the land of Canaan, they set up a heap of twelve stones to commemorate the event. A vast number of inscriptions have been gathered from the mass of ancient ruins. Of these, the following are among the most interesting: the inscription upon the pedestal of the Rostral Column of Rome; the inscription on the tombstone of the Scipios; the inscription of Zeus; the inscription termed "The Decree." This decree was engraved in three different characters. A history lost to the world has been recovered by this means. Thus you see the importance of leaving our history upon granite or marble. It will aid those in the future, in making up the history of the present.

That voice to which we have so often listened with earnest attention, is hushed forever. The country is not unmindful of his renown, or ungrateful for his services. We pause to weep at his tomb. Men die, but their words are left on record; their works remain; their example survives. He who makes a record like the one I am reviewing, he who has achieved a character like that which I now hold up to the youths of our country, may well say when the supreme hour arrives, "I am ready." While the wind sighs through the trees which shadow his grave, and the birds sing their sweet songs at the close of day, let us all remember that we too must ere long close our earthly career, and begin our lives in eternity. May our record be such that our posterity can look upon it, and truly say, "We are proud of our ancestors."

IN MEMORIAM.

Dr. JOHN McGREGOR.

Returned from prison August 3d, 1862; departed this life
November 4th, 1867.

In early morning
We watched for his coming.
Ere the first beams of day
Chased the black night away.
Fearfully, tearfully,
Under the maple tree,
In thickest dark
We watched for his coming.

Heavy the mist
Of the mid August morning.
Chilly and clammy
It rose from the valley:
A sombre pall unfurled
Over a prostrate world,
Shrouding earth, air and sky
In blackest mystery,
Filling our eyes with tears,
Chilling our hearts with fears.
As in its depth
We waited his coming,

Watched for his coming
Through mist and blackness.
From deeper misery.
Blacker captivity.
Wearisome banishment.
Sickness and languishment:
Out of a charnel house.
Loathsome, pestiferous.
Out of the depths
Of the foul Southern prisons.

Proudly we sent him
Forth on his mission:
Sadly we mourned him,
Our loved physician.
Who when war's thunder stroke
First on the nation broke.
Hurried without delay
Into the fierce affray:
On Bull Run's fatal field
Nobly disdained to yield:
Quailed not when shot and shell
Raked his frail hospital:
Urging his men to die
Rather than basely fly:
Till to captivity
Borne by the enemy:
Dragged in derision
From prison to prison.
While anxious friends in vain
Sought his release to gain:
Still interceding,
Anxiously pleading.

From Winter to Summer,
Till on this Sabbath morn
Rumors of his return
Fell upon doubting ears.
Hopes were repressed by fears,
As in the stillness,
The shuddering chillness,
The gloom and the grimness.
We watched for his coming.
Never a sound was heard,
Never word spoken;
Silence and darkness reigned
Mute and unbroken;
Till from the valley pale
A distant moaning wail
Floated o'er hill and dale.
Now sinking soft and slow,
Like summer breezes low,
Until the straining ear
Scarce a faint sigh could hear:
Then whistles loud and shrill
Echo from hill to hill,
Quinnebaug's valley thrill,
As over mead and plain
Thunders the lightning train.
We hear the warning bell
Its swift approach foretell.
With furious sally
It whistles through the valley:,
Dashing along the stream.
With frantic shriek and scream
Pausing — perchance to bring
Home the long wandering —

A moment's delay,
Then speeds far away,
Flying—like comet bright—
To viewless realms of night.

Adown the village street
Lanterns are gleaming,
Through the gray waning mist
Dark forms are stealing;
Friends, kindred, neighbors,
Together rally,
Waiting the tidings
To come from the valley:
Mutely together stood.
Hoping yet fearing,
Down the dark valley road
Anxiously peering.
Low rumbling sounds we hear.
Wagons are drawing near,
Pale spectral forms appear
Through the mist gleaming.
O'er the moist clinging soil
Slowly the horses toil.
Slow to our seeming,
Whose eager eyes intent
On those dim figures bent.
Scan every lineament,
Striving in each to trace
That dear familiar face;
Now fearing, now doubting.
Now hoping, now shouting,
"He has come! He has come!
Oh, Doctor, welcome home!

DR. JOHN McGREGOR.

From long imprisonment,
From weary banishment,
From battle, danger, chains,
Oh, welcome home again !"

We gather round him
With eager greetings,
Friend after friend
Their joy repeating;
While from sweet Thompson
    bells
A joyful chorus swells,
Ringing the glad refrain,
"Home again, home again."
Black night had passed away
Before returning day;
Vapor and cloud had gone,
Bright beamed the rising sun.
As homeward turning,
Upon this Sabbath morn.
This resurrection dawn,
No longer mourning,
But with one heart and voice
Singing "Rejoice, rejoice,"
Telling to all around
"The Lost indeed is found,
The dead is living,"
Making the Sabbath day
Where e'er the tidings stray —
At home or far away —
A glad Thanksgiving!

Five years have passed since on that morn,
That misty August morning,
Through hours of darkness and of doubt,
We watched for his returning,
And hailed our Doctor's safe release,
His happy restoration,
To freedom, practice, friends and home,
With joyful acclamation.
In deeper, darker, heavier grief,
To-day our hearts are mourning,
No friendly message cheers us now
With hopes of his returning;
No prayers, no efforts can avail
To ope that narrow prison,
No mandate can recall the dead,
Back to our yearning vision.

Yet to illume this gloomy vale
Of death and desolation,
There comes a light beyond the tomb,
A Heavenly revelation;
Death only holds the outward form,
The grave is but the portal,
Where the freed spirit drops its clay
To soar to realms immortal.
Nor can we doubt that in that realm
Beyond our dim discerning,
Were those who watched for his return
As we that Sabbath morning;
Nay, that the rapturous delight
That marked the earthly meeting
But faintly shadowed forth the joy
Of that celestial greeting.

Those who have loved him here below.
  Friends who have passed before him,
Spirits of just ones perfect grown.
  Were there rejoicing o'er him;
While the angelic hosts of God,
  In melodies supernal,
Welcomed earth's weary wanderer home
  To Sabbath rest eternal.

Eye hath not seen. nor ear hath heard.
  Nor fancy's brightest vision
Conceived the things prepared for those
  Who share the blessed elysian;
Enough. that those who honor here
  Their Saviour by confessing.
Shall be by Him acknowledged there.
  And crowned with endless blessing.

And he so deeply mourned by all.
  The much beloved physician.
Who had so nobly kept the faith.
  Fulfilled his earthly mission.
He who to those celestial heights
  Triumphantly has risen.
Perchance looks down with pity now
  On us. still bound in prison.
And when our mortal course is run.
  Our earthly fetters riven.
May we. like our departed friend.
  So faithfully have striven.
That all who welcomed his return.
  Or shared that happy meeting.
May share with him that Heavenly home.
  Receive his joyful greeting.

          Z.— *Windham County Transcript.*
Thompson. April, 1868.

THE LATE
Dr. JOHN McGREGOR.

[From the Woonsocket Patriot.]

A monument has just been erected by Mrs. Dr. John McGregor, to the memory of her lamented husband, at Phenix, R. I. It is constructed of granite from the quarry at Oneco, Conn., near his father's residence. The monument is simple, but massive in its proportions, and would seem to transmit the memory of our good doctor as long as posterity shall endure, or time shall last. The monument consists of three blocks of granite, commencing with a base of five feet in diameter and two feet thick, which, from the conformation of the ground, required sixteen horses to convey it to its resting place. The other blocks were in the same relative proportions. Above these a shaft was erected, two feet in diameter at the base and twelve feet high. The whole is a commanding structure, eighteen feet high, executed in the first style of the art. On the front of the second block of granite, the name, "Dr. John McGregor," is cut in raised letters as large as the space will admit, with his age and the date of his death underneath. Above, on the shaft, are the Masonic emblems, the Bible, on which rest the square and compass, in the degree of a Master Mason, beautifully executed. It will rear its massive height in our midst, ever recalling those welcome memories which cluster around his name, and impressing upon us the exalting thought that he has only gone up higher.

RESOLUTIONS CONCERNING

THE DEATH OF

Dr. JOHN McGREGOR.

[From the Providence Daily Journal, November 12, 1867.]

The Providence Medical Association held a meeting, last evening, by adjournment. The President, Dr. Collins, gave an interesting account of his attendance upon the international Medical Congress in Paris, and his visits to the hospitals of various European capitals. Upon motion of Dr. Gardner, a committee of three was raised to consider the matter of the running of cars through the public streets of the city, and to memorialize the City Council thereon, if it shall to the committee seem expedient. Appropriate resolutions touching the death of Dr. McGregor were

adopted, an official report of which is hereto
appended.

At a meeting of the Providence Medical
Association, held on Monday evening, Nov.
11th, the following resolutions were unanimously adopted:

WHEREAS, Our late brother, Dr. John McGregor, has, in the
Providence of God, been removed from us by sudden death:

Resolved, That we cherish in lasting esteem the many manly
and generous qualities of his character, his skill and fidelity,
which had given him a high reputation before he came among
us; his patriotism, severely tried in long captivity at the South;
his liberality to the poor, and his conscientious devotion to the
duties of his profession.

Resolved, That we keenly lament the loss of an associate who
gave promise of eminent usefulness in this city.

Resolved, That we desire to express our heartfelt sympathy
with the family that has been so suddenly and terribly bereaved.

Resolved, That these resolutions be communicated to the
widow of our late friend, and published in the Providence Daily
Journal.

G. L. Collins, M. D., President.

W. H. Traver, M. D., Secretary.

McGREGOR POST, No. 14,

G. A. R.

[From the Pawtuxet Valley Gleaner.]

Dr. John McGregor, for whom this post was named, was born October 10, 1820, on the old McGregor homestead near Greene village, Coventry, R. I. He commenced the study of medicine with Dr. William Hubbard, of Crompton, R. I., and afterwards attended lectures and graduated at the New York Medical College. After practising two years at his old home, he came to Phenix, and followed his profession here five or six years. During his stay here he was married to Miss Emily P. Ames, a daughter of the late William C. Ames. He subsequently moved to Thompson Hill, Conn., to take the place of Dr. Bowen, one of the most skillful surgeons and physicians in eastern Connecticut.

In 1861 he was appointed surgeon of the 3d Connecticut regiment, by Gov. Buckingham. He was taken prisoner at the first battle of Bull Run, and was imprisoned first in Libby Prison, Richmond; from there he was sent to Charleston, S. C., Jail; thence to Castle Pinckney, then to Columbia, in the same state; then back again to Libby; thence to Salisbury, N. C.; and finally he was taken in his weakened condition and left alone on the banks of the James river, without food, and almost naked. The second day he signalled a passing Federal steamboat, and was taken on board. He was 14 months in these prisons, and was reduced in weight from 220 to 145 pounds.

After returning home he was elected to the Connecticut Senate. But his health was so much impaired that he could not endure the long country rides necessary in the practice of his profession, and he removed to Providence. Nov. 4th, 1867, he was run over by the cars on Dyer street, in that city, and his right arm so badly crushed that amputation was necessary. He did not survive the operation. His remains were brought here, and rest beneath a handsome granite monument in a cemetery on Parker Hill, whither the veterans make an annual pilgrimage on Memorial Day.

McGregor Post, No. 8, was formed here soon after the war, but died after an enfeebled existence of five or six years. The memories of the war were fresh then, and returned soldiers did not care to be reminded of army days, so that although some twenty-five or thirty names were upon the roll at one time, it was difficult to secure the attendance of enough members to conduct the proceedings of the meeting.

The present lodge, McGregor Post, No. 14, starts under more favorable auspices. The opening meetings have been well attended. The charter members, with their army record, are as follows:

William A. Chappelle was a corporal in Co. H., 1st R. I. Cavalry, re-enlisting the 7th of November, 1861, and being discharged by reason of disability, May 17, 1862.

John Bonner was a private in Co. G., 2nd N. H. Infantry, in which he enlisted May 21, 1861, and from which he was discharged June 21, 1861, by reason of expiration of service.

Albert H. Johnson was a private in Co. H., 14th U. S. Infantry, in which he enlisted July 19, 1861, and from which he was discharged July 19, 1864. He re-enlisted in Co. A., 12th U. S. Infantry, November 29, 1867, and served a second three years.

George W. Covell served as a private in Co. E., 1st R. I. Light Artillery, from September, 1861, to January 7, 1863, he being discharged for disability. He again enlisted January 26, 1864, in Co. H., 7th R. I. Infantry, and was discharged therefrom July 13, 1865, at the close of the war.

M. A. Arnold was a private in Co. A., 9th N. Y. Cavalry, and served from September 20, 1861, to December 20, 1863. He then re-enlisted in the same company, and served as a corporal until the 17th of July, 1865.

Josiah B. Bowditch enlisted as a private in Co. D., 1st Vt. Infantry, April 20, 1861, and served till August 17, 1861, it being a three months regiment. He re-enlisted May 29, 1862, in the 9th Vt. Infantry, and served till June 24, 1865.

William H. Hopkins served as private in Co. F., 2nd R. I. Infantry, from November 23, 1864, to July 13, 1865.

Oliver P. Brown served from June 5, 1861, as private in Co. H., 2nd R. I. Infantry, until June 5, 1864.

Albert S. Luther served as private in Co. E., 3d R. I. Heavy Artillery, from August 21, 1861, to August 31, 1864, and re-enlisted in Hancock's Veteran Corps, December, 1864, serving till September, 1865.

Thomas M. Holden served as a private in the 17th Ill. Cavalry, from September 2, 1864, till May 22, 1865.

Rufus H. Northup enlisted as private in the 9th R. I. Infantry, May 26, 1862, for three months, and served till September 2, 1862.

Henry King served as assistant surgeon of the 9th R. I. (three months) Infantry, from September 2, 1862, till December 2, 1862.

John W. Hollihan served as a private in Co. E., 1st R. I. Artillery, from September 13,

1861, till the 3d of October, 1864.

Rhodes J. Colvin served as a private in Co. E., 65th N. Y. Infantry, from August 13, 1861, to December 20, 1863. He again enlisted in the 3d N. Y. Battery, December 20, 1863, and was discharged February 20, 1864, by reason of wounds received in action in front of Petersburg.

James T. Smith served as a private in Co. K., 7th R. I. Infantry, from August 8, 1861, till June 9, 1865.

John E. Sweet served as a private in the 2nd R. I. Infantry, from June 5, 1861, till June 17, 1864.

Elisha G. Tew enlisted as a private in the 12th R. I. Infantry, September 25, 1862, and served till July 29, 1863.

E. C. Capwell enlisted as a private in Co. A., 1st R. I. Cavalry, August 8, 1862, was made hospital steward, and was discharged June 6, 1865.

William Carter enlisted as a private in Co. E., 4th R. I. Infantry, September 10, 1861, and was discharged by reason of disability, October 10, 1862.

Frank M. Tucker served in the 1st R. I. Light Artillery, from September 4, 1861, till January 30, 1864. He re-enlisted in the same command, January 31, 1864, and served as a sergeant till July 16, 1865.

Arnold Lawton served in Co. F. 4th R. I. Infantry, from September 17, 1861, till March 31, 1864.

Elisha R. Watson enlisted in Co. D., 4th R. I. Infantry, August 5, 1862, and served as private till June 4, 1865.

Nathan Potter, Jr. served in the Signal Corps, from May 13, 1864, till September 5, 1865.

EXTRACTS FROM

THE

WINDHAM COUNTY TRANSCRIPT,

AUGUST 1, 1861.

[Correspondence of the Transcript.]

WASHINGTON, D. C., July 26, '61.

DEAR SIR:—You are already informed of the great fight, victory, and ignominious retreat last Sunday. I have not the time to write a description of the affair, and if I attempted to do so my pen would fail in the attempt. I passed the Sabbath, by invitation, at the house of the Hon. Amos Kendall, when we distinctly heard the cannonading, and up to 9 o'clock at night no unfavorable news reached us, but on the contrary, despatches were received stating we had won the day, which proves to be true, up to about 5 o'clock, when the teamsters took fright and commenced a stampede. This was soon communicated to the volunteers. At the same time an inconsiderate order to fall back was made, when some of the men behaved badly, though the main body fell back in good order.

The Connecticut Regiments behaved *well*, both in the fight and retreat, saving all their own baggage and equipment and that of *four* other Regiments besides.—The loss of our three Regiments is thought to be less than 100 men in killed, wounded and missing, among whom we have to record Dr. McGregor, Surgeon of the Third Regiment, supposed to be a prisoner, and James F. Wilkinson, about whom nothing has been heard from since the retreat.

The last known of Dr. McGregor, he was in the *hospital doing his duty*, and although *advised to run* it seems he preferred not to leave the poor wounded men, *even to save himself*. All honor to such heroism.

The 1st Connecticut Regiment started for home last night; and here let me say a word about the Captain of the 1st company, (I. R. Hawley, Esq.) who instead of being at the hotels, where too many officers were, I found

him with his own men, sharing with them all
the hardships of the day, and for this devotion
to their interests the men all love him. Always
esteemed, he is now loved a thousand fold
more than before. We need more such men
as Capt. Hawley.

The troops are pouring in here from the
North, and we shall soon see 150,000 men here
under McClellan, who, you may be assured,
will make the *rebels dance*.

When I learn more definitely about Dr.
McGregor and Mr. Wilkinson I will inform
you.   In great haste,

C. BLACKMAR.

Of our friend, Dr. McGregor, over whose
fate some uncertainty hangs, we cannot think
or write, save as of one who will in time be
returned to us. If a prisoner, his professional
position in the army would secure him merci-
ful treatment from any enemy raised above the
lowest dregs of barbarism—and we would not,
until compelled by the most conclusive evidence, class the Southern rebels below the
Comanche Indians. We know that he came

out unharmed from the shock of battle, and we cannot think that he has been murdered while engaged in the performance of his duties. When last seen he was busy ministering to the wants and alleviating the sufferings of the wounded, with that kindness, coolness and skill which has made him so popular among us. He was "staying with the boys," nobly and fearlessly performing his duty; and we cannot but hope that he may live to exercise, either in private or military service, that professional skill, and to manifest those qualities of mind and heart that make him so popular with his patients, and that so fit him to fill with advantage to the State, and with credit to himself, the responsible office of Surgeon in the army.

DR. McGREGOR.—From the latest reports from the Surgeon of the Third Regiment it appears that Dr. McGregor was not killed, but is a prisoner to the rebels. The news of Tuesday states that the hospitals were not burned, and that a dozen Surgeons of the Federal army are at Manassas. With every person in Windham County, we experienced a glow of pride at the heroic record of the conduct of the noble doctor. He was told that all was lost, and he must leave the field to save his life, but the impulses of a generous, humane heart were stronger than the call of self-preservation, and *he remained at his post of duty*, soothing the pains of the wounded and dying. Such self-abnegation gilds the dark cloud of our temporary defeat with rays of light from heaven. An appreciating community hope to welcome him again to his old home, where a grateful people will honor the name of McGregor forever.

SOCIETY

OF

UNION WAR PRISONERS.

Among the mementoes of the war, which
Dr. McGregor had at the time he left the
scenes of earth, to explore that unknown country from which no traveller returns, is a picture
which the doctor cherished to an extreme. To
give the reader an idea of this picture, I will
go back to a scene which took place in Charleston Jail, on December 31, 1861. At this time
the jail and jail-yard were filled with men who
had left their homes, their families, and almost
everything which makes life desirable, to
defend and uphold the flag of our nation; that
flag which cost our patriot forefathers so much
blood and suffering; a flag which they had left

untarnished to our keeping, and which we had
sworn to protect and cherish. The thought
becomes almost unbearable, when our minds
go back to December 31, 1861, and resurrect
the scenes which were then taking place in
that loathsome prison. Two hundred of our
most valiant and patriotic men were huddled
together within those walls. Men of unblem-
ished character, whose minds soared above
rebellion, whose intellects were of the highest
order, were suffering for want of bread and
many of the necessaries which sustain life.
Men who would never knowingly do a wrong
thing, and whose minds were as unbending as
the forest oak, were by fever and famine
brought to a premature grave. But amid all
their sufferings and hardships, their minds
were at work. You can imprison the body,
but you cannot confine the mind within prison
walls. The mind must be free, or it will desert
its throne. Many of our noble soldier boys
became idiotic, and died by being deprived of
food and water while in those prisons. The
doctor knew that the mind must be employed
in some way, to keep it from their terrible sit-

nation, or death would ensue; so he went to work and formed a secret organization with these brother prisoners. It was more for the purpose of keeping their minds from their sufferings than anything else, and I have heard him say that he believed that it saved his own life and many other lives.

Among those prisoners was an artist of the highest reputation. As they were moved from one prison to another, he would sketch everything within his view appertaining to the prisons. In some mysterious way his sketchings found their way within our lines, and were forwarded to Washington. President Lincoln by some means or other got hold of them. He had them enlarged, and they made a very interesting picture for those who belonged to that organization which was formed at Charleston Jail, and who were lucky enough to get once more within our lines.

I will give the reader a description of this picture. It is two feet, eight inches wide, and three feet long. It represents the different prisons and their surroundings, which those

men were in who belonged to that organization.   In the left hand corner at the top stands
Logan's tobacco factory in the city of Richmond, better known by our Northern soldiers
by the name of Libby Prison.   In the opposite
corner of the picture stands the jail at Columbia, S. C., with the jail-yards in view.   In the
center stands Castle Pinckney, S. C. The
picture is surrounded by a massive chain.
Over this prison in large type is the following:
"Union War Prisoners Association."   On the
left of the center picture stands S. C. Mill
Prison, Salisbury; and on the right another
view of the same prison is represented.   The
stagnant pool from which our poor boys got
water to quench their thirst, is in one corner
of the yard.   It makes one feel sad to look at
this picture, and remember how much suffering
there was in that prison and pen, in the time
of the war.   At the bottom of the picture
stands the City Jail, Charleston, S. C.   On the
right of the jail and in the corner is a view of
the prison-yard, and in the left hand corner is
another view.   Under the City Jail is the following in large type: "Organized in Charles-

ton Jail, December 31, 1861."

A massive chain encircles this picture, with crossed chains running from one side to the other, denoting that our boys were thoroughly guarded in those prisons. Between the views of those different prisons, are columns containing the autographs of the prisoners who belonged to that wonderful organization. I will give the names and rank as they appear upon the picture. I will commence with the left hand column, which extends from Libby Prison, which is situated in the top and left hand corner of the picture, and continues down until it comes to the view in the left hand corner at the bottom. Then I will continue column after column, until I come to the last name, which will be situated in the right hand corner at the bottom.

William H. Clark,
           2nd Lieut. Comp. G. 4th Me. Vols.

S. R. Kittredge,
           2nd Lieut. 2nd Me. Vols.

Mauniel Albaugh,
           2nd Lieut. 1st Md. Vols.

John Knoppel,
2nd Lieut. 1st Md. Vols.

Virgil T. Mercer,
2nd Lieut. 1st Md. Vols.

Robert Neely,
2nd Lieut. 1st Md. Vols.

David L. Stanton,
2nd Lieut. 1st Md. Vols.

J. C. Gregg,
Tel-Op. Hooker's Div.

A. M. Underhill,
1st Lieut. 11th N. Y. Vols.

Harry L. Perrin,
II. S. 11th N. Y. Vols.

Arnold Rummer,
1st Lieut. 68th N. Y. Vols.

Charles Wilatus,
2nd Lieut. 8th N. Y. Vols.

Frd. Mosebach,
2nd Lieut. 7th N. Y. Vols.

Albert Brands,
II. S. 68th N. Y. Vols.

Anton o. Gfrorner,
1st Lieut. 54th N. Y. Vols.

August Erhardt,
2nd Lieut. 54th N. Y. Vols.

Thos. S. Hamblin,
1st Lieut. 38th N. Y. Vols.

C. T. Gardner,
1st Lieut. 100th N. Y. Vols.

Timothy Lynch,
2nd Lieut. 100th N. Y. Vols.

John Marses,
2nd Lieut. 3d N. Y. Cav.

E. M. Raworth,
Serg't Maj. 8th Ill. Cav.

B. L. Chamberlain,
Qt. M'r 8th Ill. Cav.

H. G. Lumbard,
Adjt. 8th Ill. Cav.

G. B. Kenniston,
1st Lieut. 5th Me. Vols.

John K. Skiemer, Jr.,
1st Lieut. 2nd Me. Vols.

J. Bostwick Colony,
1st Lieut. 1st Md. Vols.

F. M. Collier,
1st Lieut. 1st Md. Vols.

Wm. E. George,
1st Lieut. 1st Md. Vols.

C. R. Gillingham,
1st Lieut. 1st Md. Vols.

Edward J. Rice,
1st Lieut. 5th Conn. Vols.

Chas. Walter,
1st Lieut. 1st Conn. Vols.

John Downey,
Capt. 11th N. Y. Vols.

Ben. Price,
Capt. 70th N. Y. Vols.

A. A. C. Williams,
Ass't Surg. 1st N. Y. Art.

Ros. A. Fish,
Capt. 32nd N. Y. Vols.

Jas. Decatur Potter,
Maj. 38th N. Y. Vols.

A. S. Cassidy,
Maj. 93d N. Y. Vols.

L. G. Camp,
Capt. 68th N. Y. Vols.

Anton Lehner,
2nd Lieut. 8th N. Y. Vols.

Oscar v. Heringon,
1st Lieut. Comp. E. 7th N. Y. Vols.

Henry Niemann,
Comm. 29th N. Y. Vols.

William Fay,
1st Lieut. 25th N. Y. Vols.

Levi Smith,
1st Lieut. 96th N. Y. Vols.

C. W. Tillotson,
1st Lieut. 99th N. Y. Vols.

M. Bailey,
Capt. 100th N. Y. Vols.

John A. Newell,
1st Lieut. 100th N. Y. Vols.

Abram H. Hasbrouck,
Adjt. 5th N. Y. Cav.

John W. Dempsey,
1st Lieut. 2nd N. Y. S. M.

Samuel Irwin,
2nd Lieut. 2nd N. Y. S. M.

F. E. Worcester,
2nd Lieut. 71st N. Y. S. M.

Geo. W. Caleff,
2nd Lieut. 11th Mass. Vols.

Leonard Gordon,
Capt. 11th Mass. Vols.

W. C. Nickels,
Comm'd Brig. B. K. Eaton.

Wm. Milhous,
Capt. 1st Va. Vols.

Timothy Swan,
1st Lieut. Comp. A. 7th Me. Vols.

James S. Baer,
1st Lieut. 1st Md. Vols.

B. H. Schley,
Capt. 1st Md. Vols.

G. W. Kugler,
Capt. 1st Md. Vols.

V. E. Von Koerber,
Capt. 1st Md. Cav.

James A. Betts,
Capt. 5th Conn. Vols.

Hiram Eddy,
Capt. 2nd Conn. Vols.

Geo. Webb Dodge,
Chap'l 11th N. Y. Vols.

C. C. Gray,
Ass't Surg. U. S. A.

Manuel C. Causten,
1st Lieut. 19th Inf. U. S. A.

W. F. Dushane,
Lt. Col. 1st. Md. Vols.

Percy Wyndham,
Col. 1st N. J. Cav.

John S. Crocker,
Col. 93d N. Y. Vols.

Lew Benedict, Jr.,
Lt. Col. 73d N. Y Vols.

Otto Botticher,
Capt. 68th N. Y. Vols.

Jos. Neustaedser,
Qt. M'r 8th N. Y. Vols.

A. H. Drake,
Capt. 33d N. Y. Vols.

Martin Willis,
Capt. 74th N. Y. Vols.

B. F. Harris,
Capt. 25th N. Y. Vols.

J. H. Nichols,
Capt. 96th N. Y. Vols.

Thomas Y. Baker,
Capt. 87th N. Y. Vols.

J. W. Dickinson,
Capt. 8th N. Y. Cav.

Amos H. White,
Capt. 5th N. Y. Cav.

James A. Farrish,
Capt. 79th N. Y. S. M.

Wm. Mandon,
Capt. 79th N. Y. S. M.

John Whyte,
1st Lieut. 79th N. Y. S. M.

P. J. Hargous,
M'rs Mate U. S. N.

J. T. Morrill,
Comm'd St. Osceola.

John McGregor,
Surg. 3d Conn. Vols.

J. D. Cruttenden,
A. Q. M. of Vols.

J. Ford Kent,
1st Lieut. 3d Inf. U. S. A.

J. Sogdes,
Maj. 1st Art. U. S. A.

O. B. Willcox,
Col. 1st Mich. Vols.

Michael Corcoran,
Col. 69th N. Y. S. M.

Geo. W. Neff,
Lt. Col. 2nd Ky. Inf.

Tim. J. Mearo,
Capt. 42nd N. Y. Vols.

John B. Hoffman,
Ass't. Surg. U. S. A.

G. H. Bean,
Capt. 1st Vt. Cav.

Mort Griffin,
Capt. 8th N. Y. S. M.

Levi S. Stockwell,
Pay Ms'r U. S. N.

Chas. H. Baker, U. S. N.,
Chief Eng. U. S. N.

L. H. Stone,
Surg. U. S. A.

Charles B. Penrose,
C. S. U. S. Vols.

D. S. Gordon,
2nd Lieut. 2nd Drag. U. S. A.

S. Bowman,
Lieut. Col. 8th Pa. Vols.

John K. Murphy,
Col. 29th Pa. Vols.

W. E. Woodruff,
Col. 2nd Ky. Inf.

R. A. Constable,
Lt. Col. 75th O. Vols.

George Austin,
Capt. 2nd Ky. Inf.

George D. Slocum,
Ass't Surg. U. S. N.

John T. Drew,
Capt. 2nd Vt. Vols.

J. P. McIvor,
Capt. 69th N. Y. S. M.

John Bagley,
1st Lieut. 69th N. Y. S. M.

Edw'd Connelly,
2nd Lieut. 69th N. Y. S. M.

James Gannon,
2nd Lieut. 69th N. Y. S. M.

E. Giddings,
2nd Lieut. 3d Wis. Vols.

Gustavus Hammer,
Capt. 3d Wis. Vols.

John J. Garvin,
Comm'd St. Union.

John H. Shohwin,
Capt. 1st N. Y. Cav.

Henry E. Clark,
Capt. 1st N. J. Cav.

W. H. Withington,
Capt. 1st Mich. Vols.

W. E. Davis,
Capt. 27th Ind. Vols.

Wm. D. Richards,
Capt. 29th Pa. Vols.

Wm. Richards, Jr.,
Capt. 29th Pa. Vols.

Cyrus Strous,
Capt. 46th Pa. Vols.

Louis Schreiner,
Chap'l 27th Pa. Vols.

W. R. Stockton,
Chap'l 61st Pa. Vols.

A. Davidson,
Capt. 11th Pa. Cav.

J. W. DeFord,
1st Lieut. Sig. Cr.

G. W. Davison,
Capt. 61st Pa. Vols.

Geo. F. Smith,
Maj. 61st Pa. Vols.

Wm. L. Curry,
Lt. Col. 106th Pa. Vols.

Thos. Clark,
Lt. Col. 29th O. Vols.

Thos. Cox, Jr.,
Capt. 1st Ky. Inf.

J. W. Sprague,
Capt. 7th O. Vols.

G. W. Shurtleff,
Capt. 7th O. Vols.

R. L. Kilpatrick,
Capt. 5th O. Vols.

H. E. Symmes,
Capt. 5th O. Vols.

James Beuse,
Capt. 6th O. Vols.

Edw'd Hayes,
Capt. 29th O. Vols.

R. B. Smith,
Capt. 29th O. Vols.

David E. Hurlburt,
Capt. 29th O. Vols.

Thos. O. Buxton,
Capt. 66th O. Vols.

J. G. Palmer,
Capt. 66th O. Vols.

M. L. Dempey,
2nd Lieut. 66th O. Vols.

J. W. Watkins,
2nd Lieut. O. Vols.

H. C. Spencer,
2nd Lieut. 3d Wis. Vols.

Isaac M. Church,
2nd Lieut. 2nd R. I. Vols.

William Luce,
Civ. Eng.

Richard H. Lee,
Capt. 6th N. J. Vols.

A. E. Welch,
1st Lieut. 1st Minn. Vols.

J. P. C. Emmons,
Capt. 1st Mich. Cav.

D. Van Buskirk,
2nd Lieut. 27th Ind. Vols.

James C. Linton,
1st Lieut. 29th Vols.

Geo. E. Johnson,
1st Lieut. 29th Pa. Vols.

M. McCarter,
1st Lieut. 93d Pa. Vols.

Sam. Cuspaden,
1st Lieut. 52nd Pa. Vols.

Wm. T. Baum,
1st Lieut. 26th Pa. Vols.

James E. Fleming,
1st Lieut. 11th Pa. Cav.

A. N. Davis,
        Capt. 3d Ky. Cav.

C. C. Keen,
        1st Lieut. 5th Ky. Cav.

Arthur T. Wilcox,
        1st Lieut. 7th O. Vols.

William N. Dick,
        1st Lieut. 5th O. Vols.

J. B. King,
        1st Lieut. 1st O. Art.

Charles Gilman,
        2nd Lieut. 6th O. Vols.

H. Gregon,
        1st Lieut. 29th O. Vols.

William Neil,
        1st Lieut. 29th O. Vols.

E. B. Woodbury,
        1st Lieut. 29th O. Vols.

B. F. Ganson,
        1st Lieut. 66th O. Vols.

W. H. Kinley,
        2nd Lieut. 6th N. J. Vols.

Frank A. Parker,
        2nd Lieut. 1st Cal. Vols.

Andrew Luke,
        2nd Lieut. 7th Ind. Vols.

Joseph Maguigin,
        2nd Lieut. 29th Pa. Vols.

J. H. Goldsmith,
        2nd Lieut. 29th Pa. Vols.

J. B. Hutchison,
2nd Lieut. 15th Pa. Vols.

J. Irwin Nerm,
2nd Lieut. 28th Pa. Vols.

E. M. Croll,
2nd Lieut. 104th Pa. Vols.

Andrew B. Wells,
1st Lieut. 8th Pa. Cav.

James Farran,
2nd Lieut. 1st Ky. Inf.

Jno. L. Walters,
2nd Lieut. 3d Ky. Cav.

James Timmous,
2nd Lieut. 5th O. Vols.

R. E. Fisher,
2nd Lieut. 5th O. Vols.

Chas. H. Robinson,
2nd Lieut. 1st O. Art.

F. S. Schieffer,
2nd Lieut. 6th O. Vols.

Thos. W. Nash,
2nd Lieut. 29th O. Vols.

Andrew Wilson,
2nd Lieut. 29th O. Vols.

Carey H. Russell,
2nd Lieut. 29th O. Vols.

W. A. Sampson,
2nd Lieut. 66th O. Vols.

I think there were two objects in forming this organization. The first was to keep their minds from their sufferings; and the second was, that, in case our army should attempt to rescue them, they might be prepared to act in concert. Many of them cling to hope as the child clings to the parent when they pass over some terrible place. Others became despondent, sunk beneath the vile waves of destitution and were lost. When hope vanished from their view, they were soon numbered with the dead.

This picture was presented to the doctor by President Lincoln or Secretary Stanton, I am not sure which. I suppose that each of the other prisoners who belonged to that organization, and who lived to come home, had one presented to him. This, with other war pictures, hangs in one of the rooms at the doctor's old homestead. It is viewed by many with much interest. Very often, when this picture is viewed by those who were in the army, pointing to some name, they will say, "I knew him. He was in our regiment," or, "He was our captain," or, "He was taken prisoner at such a battle." Those who lived to come home

were scattered from Maine to the most western states, so that in all human probability,
there were not many of them who ever met
each other after they came home. It is very
probable that the most of them have, before this
time, crossed the dark river of death, to explore
that country where we hope there will be no
rebellions or wars to agitate the mind. While
the survivors of the soldiers who rallied around
our flag and kept it from being tarnished,—
those who remain on this side of the river
which divides this from that undiscovered
country,—have their reunions, the question
arises with some, Will those poor soldiers who
have passed from earth have their reunions in
eternity? And another question often arises,
Do we, as a people, sympathize as much as we
ought with the maimed soldiers who sacrificed
so much for their country's sake, who lost their
limbs while protecting the flag which has so
long waved over one of the best and most
noble countries known on this earth? These
are questions which should be brought home
and considered.

Time's a pendulum ever swinging,
    Backward, forward, to and fro;
In its changes ever bringing,
    Mingled scenes of joy and woe!
Life is like the tides of ocean,
    One unceasing ebb and flow.
Youth advancing, age returning,
    Generations come and go.
Names remain, but things are changeful,
    Are not still what they appear.
In the name the same, this day we rally
    But where are those who once were here?
Gone to dwell 'mid scenes supernal,
    Gone beyond the world of tears;
Gone to realms undimmed, eternal,
    Gone beyond the flight of years.

Memory bless them.   Twine we garlands
    Round their graves, of festal flowers;
Requiems wail in tearful numbers,
    While advance the joyous hours

The war commenced April 12, 1861, with
the bombardment of Fort Sumter.   It virtually
ended with the surrender of Gen. Johnston
and his army, April 26, 1865, at Durham Station, Gen. Lee and his army having surren-
dered several weeks previously.

McGREGOR POST, G. A. R.,

DANIELSONVILLE, CONN.

After the tidal wave of rebellion had been broken, and that destructive element subdued, and the remaining veterans had returned to their homes, Grand Army Posts were formed in different places throughout the Northern states. One of these posts was formed in the beautiful borough of Danielsonville, Conn. It was named after Dr. John McGregor, and called McGregor Post. This showed the esteem the veterans had for him. A full history of this Post would be very interesting to many, but I have not the means at hand to give it, so I will content myself by saying that the lodge room is in keeping with the object, and adorned with many mementoes of the war.

At this time the memories of the war were fresh, and the returned soldiers seemed to enjoy themselves by assembling together and talking about the scenes which they passed through during that terrible war. Their blood would be warmed and quickened when the band played some tune which they had heard played when they were about to make a desperate charge upon those rebels; and again the soft murmurings of the beautiful Quinnebaug river would soothe their feelings, as it flowed past their lodge on its way to the grave of Uncas, the once noted chieftain of the Quinnebaug Valley.

These meetings must be pleasant in some respects, and very sad in other respects. It must be pleasant for those soldiers to meet and clasp hands with each other once more on earth, but when their minds turn back to those terrible scenes on those battle fields, they must be filled with sadness. No doubt they are willing to have the curtain drop to banish from their memory those battle field scenes where thousands of our noble young men went down

to rise no more on earth, where they bit the
earth, poured out their blood, and sacrificed
their lives for their country's sake. No doubt
many of those scenes often rise in view, but
we must hope that the cloud which appears so
dark may have a silver lining.

Time is silvering the locks of those who
remain to assemble at their lodge, and thinning
the ranks of those who suffered the hardships
and privations of that war, but there is one
consoling thought which should stimulate the
remaining comrades, and that is this—there
will be a reunion of those comrades on the
other side of the dark river of death, away
from the scenes of war and suffering, away
from the fever and the famine, away from discord and contention, where all may go and
enjoy the songs of the angels and the presence
of our Heavenly Father, where everything will
be pure and holy, in that mellow light reflected
from the throne of God. Most of their old
commanders have vanished from our sight, to
be seen no more on earth; and the time is not
far distant when those who took a part in saving our country from disgrace, will be men

who were. Their history will stand high on
the record of fame, and go down to posterity
as the sun goes down beyond the western hills,
leaving a beautiful sunset. Every young man
of to-day should be familiar with the history of
those men, and should mould his character after
their example.

When that time arrives when the last veteran
of our last war has passed from earth to join
his comrades who passed away amid the thunder and smoke of battle, and those who survived the shock of that terrible war to hear
victory proclaimed throughout our country,
then, and not until then, can our history be
complete concerning that war; for every man
has a history, and there is nothing complete
where there is any part left out. Then the
Goddess of Liberty may truly say, "I have
survived those patriots who established my
throne and protected me with their blood and
treasure for seventy-eight long years, and I
have also survived all of those valiant young
men who came to my assistance when the flag
was assailed which I have waved so long over
one of the most glorious nations on the earth.

and still my throne stands as firm as the adamantine rock, and the old flag is untarnished, with each and every star glittering in the sunlight of prosperity."

While I deeply mourn for those who have acted a noble part, and gone to assemble around a more glorious throne, the sadness is somewhat diminished by a ray of light breaking through the dark cloud, and, by its brightness, saying, "Your throne is safe, and will ever be so as long as the spirit of our forefathers exists in those who have the management of our government." May it stand until the archangel, with one foot upon the sea and the other upon the land, shall proclaim that time is no more. Then may the laurel wreath which encircles the flag of our nation be found unremoved, and in all of its freshness. This throne has stood as a sentinel over this nation for more than one hundred years. It has seen former generations rise, flourish, and pass away as if they had never existed.

Here may be seen the ruins of an Indian empire; and though they were the children of the forest, and though they left no monuments of sculpture, painting, or poetry, yet great were they in their fall, and sorrowful is the story of their wrongs. They once had cities, but where are they now? It is true they worshipped the Great Spirit, and the genius of storm and darkness. The sacred pages of revelation had never been unrolled to them, and the gospel of our Savior had never sounded in the ears of the poor children of the forest. They heard the voice of their God in the morning breeze; they saw Him in the dark clouds that rose in wrath from the west. Here they once lived and loved. Here the council fire blazed and the war-whoop echoed among their native hills. But at length the white man from the east came upon their shores. They yielded not their empire tamely, but they could not stand against the sons of light, and so they fled.

To-day America opens wide the gate and smooths the way by which the aspiring youth of our land may drink at the fountain of freedom, and if they will follow those who have left in our keeping the greatest treasure on earth, and who are beckoning us onward, the day is not far distant when the bar, the senate,

and the pulpit will re-echo the principles upon
which our government stands, and will draw
the eyes of all learned men from beyond
Atlantic's waves to the growing blessings of
the American republic. A noble feeling has
already been awakened throughout the Union.
Offerings from the treasury of almost every
state have already been laid on the altar, and
consecrated to the elevation of man. The
poet's muse, the orator's eloquence, and the
historian's pen, will erelong be employed on
nobler themes than even our majestic rivers,
matchless water-falls, interminable forest, or
smiling prairies — the cultivation of human
intellect, the elevation of the human mind
above all Grecian and all Roman fame. This
country is raising a monument that will last
when the names and the memories of thousands
of men and things that are now occupying a
large share of public notice shall have passed
into oblivion. The sparks of intelligence
which are scattered among us will kindle a
fire, which, if rightly consecrated, will give
stability to the altars of religion and liberty,
and shed a brighter halo around our national

character than all the achievements of armies or of navies. To these enlightened and noble efforts, every patriot should bid God speed, and, in the sphere in which he moves, second the efforts to induce the rising hopes of our country to prepare themselves for the varied duties that their country may require them to discharge.

THE DOCTOR'S PARENTS.

The writer, having neglected to give a short account of Jeremiah McGregor, father of Dr. John McGregor, in its proper place will give it here.

In 1780, one hundred and six years ago, the father of Dr. John McGregor was born.

In 1800, he with fourteen others, was employed by government, to survey and lay out certain townships in the state of New York. He was in the government employ two years. At that time, fever and ague was so prevalent in that section, that very few could remain more than a short time. A large portion of the state of New York was a wilderness, inhabited only by Indians. The Mohawks, the Tonawandas, and the Oneidas,

roamed through the interior. There were no
canals or railroads then. The usual mode of
emigration was to carry the family and household goods in canvas-covered wagons, drawn
by oxen. The toilsome journey was made
along rough roads, through dark forests, and
across rapid streams. Not a single state had
been formed out of the extensive region called
the North-West Territory, lying between the
Alleghany and the Rocky mountains. It was
at one time claimed by the French, under the
name of Louisiana. A large portion of this
rich country was the wide hunting ground of
the Indians. The celebrated Tecumseh was
the mighty chief and warrior farther west.

A man by the name of Elliot was the head
engineer; and many of his lines and plats are
referred to at this distant day. They surveyed
and platted the Holland Purchase, or what is
better known as Batavia, and another township
west of Saratoga.

After returning home, he assisted his father
in farming, and in the hotel business, until his
father gave up the business, when he continued
in the same line of business for over sixty long

years.

In 1812, the war with England threw the country into excitement, and unsettled, to some extent, its business. At that time, he was colonel of the ninth regiment of militia. The following was his commission from Gov. Jones.

By his excellency, William Jones, Esq., Governor, Captain-General, and Commander-in-Chief, of the State of Rhode Island and Providence Plantations.

To JEREMIAH McGREGOR, Esq.: Greeting.

You, the said Jeremiah McGregor, having been elected by the General Assembly, at the session on the first Wednesday of May instant, to the Office of Colonel of the ninth Regiment of Militia in the State aforesaid, are hereby, in the Name of the State of Rhode Island and Providence Plantations, authorized, empowered and commissioned, to exercise the Office of Colonel of the Regiment aforesaid, and to command and conduct the same, or any part thereof. And in case of an Invasion, or Assault of a common Enemy, to infest or disturb this State, you are to alarm and gather together said Regiment under your Command, or such Part thereof as you shall deem sufficient; and therewith, to the utmost of your Skill and Ability, you are to resist, expel and destroy them, in order to preserve the Interest of the good Citizens of this State. You are also to follow such Instructions and Orders as shall, from Time to Time, be given forth, either by the General Assembly, the Governor and General Council, or other your Superior Officers. And for your so doing, this Commission shall be your sufficient Warrant and Discharge.

Given under my Hand, and the Seal of the State, this Eleventh Day of May, in the Year of our Lord, One Thousand Eight Hundred and Twelve, and in the Thirty-Sixth Year of Independence.

By his Excellency's Command.

WILLIAM JONES.

SAMUEL EDDY, Secretary.

The following September, he was ordered to call out his regiment, and wait for further orders. He obeyed the order by calling his regiment out, on the plain just east of a hotel located where the Coventry Asylum now stands. At that time, it was expected that the regiment would be called to Newport, but on the second day orders came for the regiment to be dismissed with the understanding that they should hold themselves in readiness at a minute's warning; but no further orders came. The war after a while fizzled out; but not until it had done much damage to our commerce, and disorganized many branches of our business. For a long time, all of our merchandise was transported from Boston to New York, and *vice versa*, with ox teams. Our young men of to-day would think it quite an undertaking to drive an ox team from Boston to New York and back; but at that time we had young men who could, and were willing to do it. I have no doubt that we have young men to-day, who, if it was necessary, would do it without murmuring, for the last war demonstrated, beyond a doubt, that our young men were willing to sacrifice as much as any young men of any nation, or at any period.

In 1831, the doctor's father took down the old sign which had swung before the old hotel for fifty long years; and when he raised it again it had been repainted, and so wonderfully changed that many of the beholders were astonished. The portrait of Washington had been changed for the picture of a young and noble looking horse, trampling beneath his feet an object which he seemed anxious to destroy. By his side stood a young and fearless looking man, who seemed to be urging him on. Over his head waved a banner with the word "Temperance" in gilt letters, and underneath was the proprietor's name, with the date 1831.

At this time, the cause of temperance was in its infancy; and it was not strange that many at that day were surprised at seeing the old sign so much changed. They soon discovered that the interior of the hotel was as much changed as the old sign. The shelves in the bar, on which usually stood decanters filled with all kinds of alcoholic liquors, were perfectly empty. No signs of alcoholic beverage were to be seen. Many were discomforted, and some showed their displeasure by tearing the sign down a number of times; but it arose as often as it fell. After a while the people became more reconciled, and the old sign was allowed to swing to and fro without molestation. From 1831, the hotel was kept on strictly temperance principles. I think that I am safe in saying that this was the first temperance sign ever raised in Rhode Island.

In 1841, he joined the Christian Baptist Church, at Rice City; and ever after was a consistent member of that church.

He was buried in the family cemetery on the old homestead, where his father and mother, his wife and two brothers, in dreamless sleep, are waiting for the resurrection morn.

As I said in the commencement, Dr. John McGregor's mother was the daughter of Major Jonathan Nichols; and I might justly say that the doctor owed much of what he was to his mother. That person never lived in Coventry, who read more, or remembered more of what they read, than the doctor's mother. She always kept well posted on all matters concerning the welfare of our country. She seldom gave advice until she had thoroughly examined the matter, and her advice was always in the right direction. Her sufferings while the doctor was in prison were intense; and when his life was sacrificed in Providence, her mind was almost dethroned. She loved her children as none but a mother could. She always endeavored to bend the twig in the right direction, for she believed that the way the twig was bent, the tree would be inclined.

THE
McGREGOR HOMESTEAD.

[From the Pawtuxet Valley Gleaner.]

We wander all through the old mansion. We look at the old furniture which has been in the family over a century. We hear the old clock ticking, that has stood in one place eighty long years. We see Col. John McGregor's old regimentals which he wore in the Continental Army in 1776, and the old sword still hangs upon the wall, which he unsheathed at the battle of Bunker Hill, and sheathed at New York when Washington dismissed his army. We see his old muster roll dated October 11, 1776 to Nov. 25, 1783, with the names of those patriots who were under his command. We see orders from Washing-

ton, Durkee, and from other commanders.
We see files of old papers which were printed
in Rhode Island when Washington was president: the first Chronicles, the first Journal,
the first American, and the first Patriot ever
printed in Rhode Island. We see autographs
of many noted men, such as Governors
William Jones, John B. Francis, Gov. Jackson, John Clark, Albert C. Greene, James
F. Simmons, Joseph S. Tillinghast, John
Whipple, William Anthony, and a thousand
others. We read on a pane of glass in one of
the windows a verse inscribed by Gen. Lafayette in 1825. We see an organ brought from
foreign lands in 1708, the only one of the kind
in the United States. In the attic stands the
old loom, the linen wheel, the hetchel, and
many of those things which were very necessary one hundred years ago.

This house was once a center of busy interest, and is located twenty-two miles from
Providence and twenty-three miles from Norwich on the Providence and Norwich turnpike.
For over a century a hotel was kept here by
the McGregors. The old sign that swung

before the house one hundred years ago to advertise the business there transacted, is in the house still.

We enter the Masonic Lodge room which is in the west part of the house. Seventy years ago the Hamilton Lodge was instituted in this room and was the first offspring of Manchester Lodge. As we enter this room silence is upon the walls. The craftsmen are not here. The master's gavel is silent, and the square and compass stand out in bold relief as much as to say, " We encompass the whole and square the end of time." We see on the wall autographs of some of the crafts- men. We see the old inkstand, long since dry, and here are still to be seen things that will remind us of the past. Peace to the name of the old Lodge room. Silence is upon thy walls, proud room, for a memorial. Such is the old Hamilton Lodge room, a magnificent relic.

Col. John McGregor came from Dundee, Scotland. He brought to this country Ma- sonic seed and planted it at Anthony, R. I. It germinated and grew. The results attained are well known to the fraternity.

He raised a company of volunteers in the town of Plainfield, Conn., and on the sixth of June, 1775, they left Plainfield and marched for Boston. Many of that company never returned. When the sun rose on that memorable 17th of June, 1775, that little band of patriots was diligently at work fortifying Bunker Hill. Let us draw a vail over that bloody scene and leave to the imagination of the reader the sacrifice that was made that day. Let it suffice.

When Warren went down, Freemasonry lost one of its most brilliant stars. The ring of the fraternity seemed to be broken. The craft generally rejoice in being known as a fraternity, the limits of which are like a ring that is without beginning or end, being one continuous circle; such, of course, is Masonry, according to its teachings, and should be in fact. It could, and ought to be, and if the brethren only took the pains to make it, it would be so.

I have wandered from the old homestead. I will now go back. The reader may ask why I call it the old McGregor Homestead. I will

tell you. Five generations of McGregors
have lived here, Col. John McGregor, Jeremiah, son of Col. John, Dr. John, son of
Jeremiah and grandson of Col. John, John
the 3d, great-grandson, and Virgil Johnson,
great-grandson of Jeremiah and great-great-
grandson of Col. John McGregor. Jeremiah,
father of Dr. John, lived here 95 years. Jeremiah S. McGregor still lives at the old
homestead. What a consolation it must be to
know that your parents, grandparents, great-
grandparents and great-great-grandparents
have lived in the same house, slept in the same
rooms, walked the same paths, drank from the
same well, read the same papers, and used the
same furniture.

And what is home and where, but with the loving?
 Happy thou art that so canst gaze on thine!
My spirit feels but in its weary roving,
 That with the dead, where'er they be, is mine.

Ask where the earth's departed have their dwelling,
 Ask of the clouds, the stars, the trackless air:—
I know it not,—yet trust a whisper, telling
 My lonely heart that love unchanged is there.

                                COSMOPOLITE.

REMINISCENCES

OF

ANCIENT PLAINFIELD.

[Copied From a Connecticut Paper.]

Let us go back to 1774; at this time the
Colonies were in a turmoil from end to end,
by reason of a threatened Coercion Bill, a bill
designed by Great Britain to put down the
Colonies and their just claims of Fixity of
Tenure for the people. The public excitement
continued to increase. Associations were
formed in many places throughout the Colonies, under the title of Sons of Liberty. Such
an association was formed in Plainfield.

Previous to said date a man from Dundee,
Scotland, by the name of John McGregor,
located in said town. He soon made many
acquaintances in Plainfield, and erelong be-

came acquainted with Israel Putnam, of Brooklyn. McGregor was well posted in military discipline, having seen much service in Scotland; and as Putnam had seen something of war, their hearts beat in union. McGregor was selected to discipline said association in the arts of war.

On the 19th of April, 1775, was shed at Lexington, the first blood in the Revolutionary war. At this, the Sons of Liberty communicated with each other by signals. The beacon lights, located on many of the lofty hills, were strictly attended to.

On the evening of June 6th, the beacon light on Shepard's Hill was seen streaming heavenward. It was the signal for the Sons of Liberty to assemble at their headquarters. Said headquarters were at Simeon Shepard's residence, which was located where the Plainfield almshouse now stands.

On the following day there was great excitement in Plainfield. They all knew that the association would soon have news from Boston. About two o'clock in the afternoon, a horseman was seen coming at breakneck speed, from towards Boston. The assembly was spellbound as the messenger dashed up to the headquarters. The man was as pale as death. He was completely exhausted, and was taken from his horse and carried into the house. The poor horse trembled and reeled, and before the dispatch could be unlashed from the saddle, he fell to the ground. He had carried his last message. The dispatch was directed to John McGregor. The following is a copy.

BOSTON, June 6th, 1775.

CAPTAIN JOHN McGREGOR: Dear Sir,— Forward your men to Boston as soon as possible. They will be needed soon.

Your friend,

ISRAEL PUTNAM.

The following night was a busy and sleepless one for the men and women in Plainfield, for the company was to commence its march for Boston at seven o'clock the next morning. At the appointed time, those Sons of Liberty formed themselves into line, and waited for the word, "Forward!" Swift as the summons came, they left the plow mid-furrow, standing still, the half ground corn-grist in the mill, the spade in the earth, the ax in cleft. They went where duty seemed to call. They only knew they could but die. They had not long to wait for the word, "Forward," for erelong McGregor came to the front, unsheathed the sword which had been presented to him by the association, and, in a clear voice, said, "Sons of Liberty! all of you who are willing to share with me the dangers and sufferings of war, for your country's sake, Forward March!" Not one faltered.

The reader can imagine the feelings of the friends of these young men, as they left Plainfield, and wound their way over the hills and through the valleys, until they reached Boston.

On the 9th, this little band of patriots filed into one of the redoubts near Boston. Putnam was there ready to receive them. On the 17th, they took an active part in the battle of Bunker Hill. Some of these men served until Washington disbanded his army at New York. Many of them never returned to Plainfield. We will draw a vail over Vailey Forge, Trenton, Morristown, White Plains, and many other places, where their sufferings can never be fully described.

The old sword which John McGregor had, presented to him by said association, and which he used all through the war, is now in possession of the writer. Also, his old muster roll containing the names of the men in his company. His company was in Col. John Durkee's regiment. For the benefit of the posterity of those patriots, I will transcribe a part of that old muster roll. Space will not allow me to copy the whole roll, therefore the reader must be content with a part. The following are some of the names found on said roll:

James M. Daniels, John Sanders, Clear Haymont, Joshua Stoddard, Henry Shaw, Solomon Haymont, Samuel Stafford, Abel Franklin, Josiah Hogers, Philemon Love, Asa Law, Oliver Hogers, John Williams, Lot Chace, Reuben Bryant, Caesar Steward, William Glenn, Therea Durkee, Ames Bennett, Pomp Haymont, Peter Horry, Jedediah Brown, James Dike, John Almey.

The grave of Putnam should be immortalized; men die, but their works remain, their example survives.

To-day, this republic holds in secure grasp,

every element of power, every condition of existence. Firm and strong, she extends to other nations the hand of friendship. We have erected upon our shores a statue of Liberty illuminating the world. We cannot be deaf, we must not be blind, to her munificence. The centennial anniversary draws on apace. The national spirit is revived. The national wealth, and power, and pride, are at their zenith.

When the July sun shall hereafter rise in its perennial course, may its morning rays, as they lift from the Atlantic waves, gild the spotless shaft which shall stand for countless ages, the witness of a nation's gratitude; and as they fall upon each patriot's grave, and finally sink in effulgence in the deep bosom of the Pacific ocean, may we remember, and our children and children's children after us remember, the obligations we owe those patriots for our establishment and security in this vast heritage.

SKETCH

OF

DR. P. K. HUTCHINSON.

The subject of this sketch, Dr. P. K. Hutchinson, was born on the 29th of August, 1817, in the town of Plainfield, in the state of Connecticut. The early youth of Dr. Hutchinson was spent in the beautiful village of Plainfield, and almost within the shadows of that ancient academy, in which so many noted men, fifty years ago, acquired their education. He entered that academy very early in life and continued until he graduated. Being strongly inclined to study, he sought every opportunity for improving his mind, and a profession was the great end at which he aimed. After leaving the old academy at Plainfield, he entered

Amherst College, where he remained until he graduated with the highest honors. After he left the college, he immediately entered the office of Dr. Coggeshall, an eminent physician, then residing in Plainfield, and commenced the study of medicine. He subsequently graduated at the Medical University at New Haven.

In 1847, he opened an office and located himself in Coventry, Rhode Island, taking the place vacated by Dr. John McGregor, who had moved to Phenix. For twenty years he remained at the old McGregor homestead. In 1850, he married Miss Jane McGregor, daughter of Jeremiah McGregor and sister to Dr. John McGregor.

He soon acquired a reputation as a physician of the highest order. His practice at this time was very extensive, and his success as physician was beyond what he had ever hoped. He had gained the confidence of the people, and his reputation was fully established. He had previously joined the Christian Baptist Church, at Rice City, and was a very active member. He took a great interest in the common school

system, and did very much toward the furtherance of the cause. He was always ready and
willing to assist in any work which would
improve the morals of the people, or raise them
to a more exalted position. He was generous
to an extreme. He was just as ready and willing to doctor the poor as he was the rich. The
beggar never went from his house empty-
handed. He was what you might call a whole-
souled man.

Subsequently, he purchased a farm at Rice
City, and moved thither. He was elected to
many offices in the town and state. For a
long time he was one of the town's School
Committee, and for two years represented
Coventry in the State Legislature.

In 1862, he was appointed assistant surgeon
of the twelfth Rhode Island regiment, commanded by Col. George H. Brown. At the
battle of Fredericksburg, he, with other doctors, was in one of the churches occupied as
a hospital. Soon after this battle, he was
taken with chronic diarrhœa, and was obliged
to resign his office and return home.

He devoted much of his time to extending

a gracious hospitality to his friends. But the
day was fast approaching when his earthly
labors were to cease. It was not long before
his illness had rapidly increased, and his condition was such that physicians entertained no
hope of his recovery. He also was sensible
that his last days were very near. With the
most perfect calmness, he conversed with his
family and friends, and gave directions concerning his funeral, being desirous that his last
resting-place on earth should be in the family cemetery, on the old McGregor homestead.
Gradually, he was sinking; and on October
31st, he inquired the day of the month. Being
told that it was the 31st of October, he told
his friends that he might live till another day,
and expressed an earnest wish that he might.
His prayer was heard. The dawn of another
day broke upon his eyes, and then they were
closed forever. And what a noble consummation of a noble life! To die where his name,
by his own acts, stood high on the record of
fame, was glorious; to die amid the people who
looked up to him as the author under God of
their greatest blessings, was all that was

wanted to fill up the record of his life. Fifty-
five summers had rolled over his head. He
had passed the meridian of his usefulness, and
his departure was similar to a beautiful sunset.
His spirit was freed from the bondage of earth,
as it left the scenes of his earthly honors.

In him, the elements of self control were
strong. Possessing great fortitude, as well as
personal courage, his command of temper was
such that his friends seldom saw him in a pas-
sion. He was also possessed of simplicity of
manner, although coupled with easy dignity.
He was fluent and eloquent in conversation,
and remarkably precise and correct in his
language. As a classical scholar, his writings
were after the best models of antiquity, and
he never endeavored to convince by the mere
force of argument. So nearly the whole of
Dr. Hutchinson's life was passed before the
public, that his actions speak his character
better than words can express them, and whatever his faults may have been, if he had them,
his name will be cherished, and he will be held
in grateful memory, as one of our most eminent
physicians.

He died at his home, in Rice City, November 1st, 1872, aged 55 years. At his death, the Rice City Church lost a worthy member, and the community a skillful physician. Rev. Mr. Westgate, from Phenix, preached a very instructive and interesting discourse upon the occasion, taking for his text, the 7th and 8th verses found in the fourth chapter of the second Epistle of Paul, the Apostle, to Timothy, "I have fought a good fight, I have finished *my* course, I have kept the faith: Henceforth there is laid up for me a crown of righteousness, which the Lord, the righteous judge, shall give me at that day: and not to me only, but unto all them also that love his appearing."

A massive granite monument denotes the place where the mortal part of Dr. P. K. Hutchinson is peacefully resting. There is nothing certain in this life but death.

Leaves have their time to fall,
And flowers to wither at the North wind's breath,
And stars to set — but all,
Thou hast *all* seasons for thine own, O Death!

CONCLUSION.

For the benefit of our posterity, and to aid the historians who, in the future, will doubtless endeavor to make their histories of this nation as complete as possible, we should exert ourselves in gleaning and preserving everything which will be interesting and useful to the succeeding generation. Every nation has a history; and the completeness depends upon how much the historian can find preserved to form said history.

> Little drops of water.
> Little grains of sand,
> Make the mighty ocean,
> And the beauteous land.

Every man has two histories, a public and a private one. The one becomes fairly the property of the public, by virtue of his having been connected with events in which everyone has a share of interest; but the other belongs exclusively to himself, his family, and his intimate friends. Our most lofty mountains are formed and composed of small particles of quartz, feldspar, mica, different kinds of ore, and many other things too numerous to mention, which it takes to make those mighty elevations. The Amazon river, the largest, but not the longest, river in the world, is formed and made complete by the contribution of hundreds of other smaller rivers; and those rivers are formed by thousands of little brooks, contributing their waters; and those little brooks are formed by thousands and thousands of tiny springs of water, located in different places on the east side of the Andes Mountains, hundreds of miles apart. So it is with history. It is made complete by the small particles which the historian gleans, and which he finds scattered in different localities. To make history reliable, scenes should be described by those who witnessed them, places should be described by those who have seen them, the acts of men should be described by those who know the facts, the sayings of men should be repeated by those who heard those sayings, and a record should be made of the testimony of those witnesses. It is not so very strange that historians disagree in their accounts of scenes which they describe, from the fact that witnesses located in different positions, view scenes in a different light. There is no excuse for historians disagreeing on dates, names, and the general facts. Mistakes will occur with the most correct writers, and it proves that man is imperfect in many ways. It is not given to man to achieve perfection; else this world would not be a state of discipline.

Why is it that we are so very particular about having all of our deeds, wills, contracts, and many of our business transactions, recorded, and those records placed in some secure depository, for preservation. The whole object is this; our memory being fallible, if we make a record of our acts and doings, and those records are preserved, we can refer to those records and ascertain the facts, and the succeeding generation may have the benefit of those records, after we are gone from earth.

History is nothing more nor less than the record of the past. Men die, but their record remains, their example survives. When I look back over the period of fifty years, crowded with great events, and which has witnessed the convulsion of the nation, the reorganization and reconstruction of our political system,— when in my mind's eye I people this country with those whose forms have been familiar to me, whose names, many of them historical names, are now carved on granite or marble that covers their dust, I am filled with a sadness inexpressible, yet full of consolation; for, musing on the transitory nature of all sublunary things, I come to perceive that their instability is not in their essence, but in the forms which they assume, and in the agencies that operate upon them; and when I recall those whom I have seen fall around me, and whom I thought necessary to the success, almost to the preservation, of great principles, I recall also those whom I have seen step into the vacant places, put on the armor which they wore, lift the weapons which they wielded, and march on to the consummation of the work which they inaugurated. And thus I am filled with reverent wonder at the beneficent ordering of nature, and inspired with a loftier faith in that Almighty Power without whose guidance and direction all human effort is vain, and with whose blessing the humblest instruments that He selects are equal to the mightiest work that He designs.

When we contemplate the close of life, the termination of man's designs and hopes, the silence that now reigns among those who a little while ago were so busy or so gay, who can avoid being touched with sensations at once awful and tender? What heart but then warms with the glow of humanity? In whose eye does not the tear gather, on revolving the fate of passing and short-lived man? Of all the sorrows which we are here doomed to endure, none is so bitter as that occasioned by the fatal stroke which separates us, in appearance, forever, from those to whom either nature or friendship had intimately joined our hearts. Memory from time to time renews the anguish, opens the wound which seemed once to have been closed, and, by recalling joys that are

past and gone, touches every spring of painful
sensibility. In these agonizing moments, how
relieving the thought that the separation is
only temporary, not eternal; that there is a
time to come of reunion with those with whom
our happiest days were spent, whose joys and
sorrows once were ours, whose piety and virtue
cheered and encouraged us, and from whom,
after we shall have landed on the peaceful
shore where they dwell, no revolutions of
nature shall ever be able to part us more. Such
is the society of the blessed above. Of such
is the multitude composed which stands before
the throne.

THE END.